Heinrich Heine, Theodore Martin

Poems and Ballads

Second Edition

Heinrich Heine, Theodore Martin

Poems and Ballads
Second Edition

ISBN/EAN: 9783744782258

Printed in Europe, USA, Canada, Australia, Japan

Cover: Foto ©Andreas Hilbeck / pixelio.de

More available books at **www.hansebooks.com**

POEMS AND BALLADS

BY

HEINRICH HEINE

DONE INTO ENGLISH VERSE

BY

SIR THEODORE MARTIN, K.C.B.

SECOND EDITION

WILLIAM BLACKWOOD AND SONS
EDINBURGH AND LONDON
MDCCCLXXXII

L'ENVOI.

THE genius of Heine is only to be appreciated by the study of his very copious poetical works, as well as of his voluminous prose. But to the mass of readers he will always be chiefly known by his 'Book of Songs.' There are few whose experience is either so wholly happy or so wholly sad that they will not find in these an echo of some of the deepest emotions they have known;—few so deadened to the charm of exquisite fancies clothed in exquisite language that they will not willingly surrender themselves to be swayed at will by these consummate specimens of the poet's "so potent art." Most of the lyrics in the 'Book of Songs' need no other music than their own. Nevertheless, many of them have been wedded to melodies

not unworthy of their beauty by the genius of
Schubert, Mendelssohn, Schumann, and others.
Thus, their fascination has been in some degree
heightened for those whose love of music is equal
to their love of poetry, and in this way also they
have been made familiar to a public whom they
might not otherwise have reached.

The present Volume contains translations of all
the songs and ballads in the 'Book of Songs' which
the translator ventures to think are likely to be
acceptable to an English reader. Perhaps a severe
criticism would even say that the principle of ex-
clusion might have been carried further. Heine,
like most poets, wrote too much; and his name
would rank higher in the world of letters if many
of his pieces, which are either steeped in grossness
or deformed by a revolting cynicism, had never
seen the light. In his selections, the translator's
object has been to show the poet at his best, and
at the same time to illustrate the cynicism and
bitter irony which are as characteristic of Heine
as are his passion, his pathos, his picturesque sim-
plicity and force. Some of the pieces, which have
been added from his miscellaneous poems, are less
generally known, but they are no less impressed

with the distinctive qualities of the poet's genius than the poems of the 'Book of Songs.'

The warm welcome given to many of these translations, as they appeared from time to time in 'Blackwood's Magazine,' has induced the translator to add to their number, and to include them in a volume, which he trusts may not be unwelcome even where the originals are best known.

INDEX.

PAGE

PREFACE TO THIRD EDITION OF THE BOOK OF SONGS, 1

YOUTH'S SORROWS.

DREAM PICTURES.

I have had dreams of wild love wildly nursed, . . .	7
A dream that eerie was to see, ...	8
One night—'twas in a dream—myself I spied, . . .	13
I saw in dream a dapper mannikin, ...	14
What sets my blood so mad a-spin?	15
In sweetest dream, at dead of night, ...	18
I slept,—my sleep was soft and sweet, ...	22

SONGS.

Thou, so fair, so pure of guile, ...	24
When I am with my dearest dear, ...	25
I at morn get up, and " Will she, ...	26
Alone with the anguish that tore me, ...	27
Lay your dear little hand on my heart, my fair ! . .	28
Oh, if these songs of mine were, ...	29
Oh, fair cradle of my sorrow, ...	30
Tower and castled peak look downward, ...	32
In my lonely first despair, it, ...	33
Where above the stars are glowing, ...	33
With roses and cypress and tinsel gold, ...	34

ROMANCES.

A horseman rode sadly up the glen, ... 36
Hans and Gretel wheel and dance, ... 37
When my grandam bewitch'd Betty Grimes, the folk, . . 39
For France two grenadiers held their way, ... 40
Up, boot and saddle, my boy! Bestride, ... 42
I go not alone, fair lady mine, ... 43
The midnight hour was drawing on, ... 44
Each wave I counted, as I stood, ... 47
I see her still, that fair enchantress, ... 48
When spring with the sunny days comes in, . . . 50

LYRICAL INTERMEZZO.

'Twas in the glorious month of May, ... 53
Sweet flowers spring up, the fairest, ... 54
The rose, the lily, the sun, and the dove, . . . 54
Whene'er I look into thine eyes, ... 55
Thy face, so sweet and fair to see, ... 56
Thy cheek incline, dear love, to mine, ... 57
I will steep my fainting spirit, ... 58
Immovable, unchanging, ... 59
Oh, I would bear thee, my love, my bride, . . . 60
The lotus-flower is scared by, ... 61
My love you cannot, cannot brook, ... 62
Oh, swear not, only kiss me now, ... 63
Say, love, art thou not a vision, ... 64
Fair she is as foam-born Venus, ... 65
I am not wroth, my own lost love, although, . . . 66
Yes, thou art wretched, and I am not wroth, . . . 67
Hark to yon fiddling and fluting, ... 68
And hast thou forgotten, so fickle thou art, . . . 69
If the little flowers knew how deep, ... 70
Why are the roses so wan of hue, ... 71
They told thee much, much they invented, . . . 72
The linden blossomed, the nightingale sung, . . . 73
A mighty to-do with each other we made, . . . 74

And as I linger'd so many a day, ... 75
The violets blue of those eyes of thine, ... 76
The world is so fair, and the sky so blue, ... 76
When thou shalt lie, my darling, low, ... 77
A pine-tree stands alone on, ... 78
Stars, that bright and golden are, ... 78
Oh, were I but the footstool, where, ... 79
Since my love did me beguile, ... 80
Tomfools in their Sunday clothes ramble, . . . 81
Shape after shape uprises, ... 82
Friendship, Love, the Philosopher's Stone, . . . 83
A young man loves a maiden, ... 84
When I hear the song, that erst 85
The flowers all turn their gazes, ... 86
I dreamt of a monarch's daughter fair, ... 87
My love, we were sitting together, ... 88
From the realm of old-world story, ... 89
I loved thee, and oh, I love thee still, ... 90
'Tis summer, a bright summer morning, ... 91
My love in its shadowy glory, ... 92
People have teased and vex'd me, ... 93
'Tis summer, fiery summer, ... 94
When it comes to lovers' parting, ... 95
My songs, they are poison'd—poison'd ! . . . 96
Again the old dream came back to me, . . . 97
I stand on the mountain summit, ... 98
My carriage rumbles slowly, ... 99
In dreams, oh, I have wept, love ! 100
I see thee nightly in dreams, my sweet, . . . 101
Hark to the roar and the howling, ... 102
The autumn wind rustles the tree-tops, . . . 103
A star is falling, falling, ... 104
The Dream-god bore me to a giant keep, . . . 105
The midnight was cold, and still, and sad, . . . 106
At the cross-roads a wretch is buried, ... 107
Where'er I be, a darkness stronger, ... 108
Upon my eyes lay midnight, ... 109
The old unhappy ditties, ... 112

THE RETURN HOME.

Once upon my life's dark pathway, ... 117
I wist not what it is daunts me, ... 118
My heart, my heart is heavy, ... 120
I roam through the wood heavy-hearted, ... 122
The night, it is damp and stormy, ... 123
When I stumbled by chance in a journey, ... 125
We sat by the fisherman's cottage, ... 127
My bonnie blithe fisher-maiden, ... 129
The moon is up, and shining, ... 130
The moon, a giant orange, rests, ... 131
In grey folds of cloud enveloped, ... 132
The wild wind draws his breeches on, ... 133
The gale tunes up for a revel, ... 134
The twilight has died in darkness, ... 135
When past thy house at morning, ... 137
The sea loomed wide, a shining flat, ... 138
On the verge of the far horizon, ... 139
So again I am pacing the well-known streets, . . . 140
Into yon halls I stept, ... 140
Still is the night, and the streets are lone, . . . 141
Sleep, and in peace? How canst thou? 142
The girl is asleep in her chamber, ... 143
I stood on her picture gazing, ... 144
I a most ill-starr'd Atlas! I am doom'd, ... 145
Years come and go; generations, ... 146
I had a dream; the moon looked drear, ... 147
What's this? A tear, one only? 148
The waning autumn moon looks, ... 149
'Tis the very roughest of weather, ... 151
People think, for love I am wasting, ... 152
Oh, if thy white lily fingers, ... 153
Has she never, then, given token, ... 154
They both were in love, but neither, ... 155
When I told you my troubles, my tale of despair, . . 155
My bairn, we aince were bairnies, ... 156
My heart is sad, with sore misgiving, ... 158

As the moon through clouds that darkle, . . . 159
In a dream I saw my darling, ... 160
Heart, heart mine, no longer vex thee, ... 162
Thou art even as a flower is, ... 163
Child! it would be your undoing, ... 164
When abed I lie enfolded, ... 165
Lassie with the lips sae rosy, ... 166
Fathoms deep may drift the snow, ... 167
What I suffer for love can you, ... 167
I wanted to linger about you, ... 168
Yes! sapphires are those eyes of thine, ... 169
I have racked my brain this many a day, ... 170
They have company coming this evening, ... 171
Oh, would all the anguish I suffer, ... 172
Pearls hast thou and diamonds, dearest, ... 173
July was quite at its best when I left you, ... 174
Alone through the dark we travelled, ... 175
Like ghosts in a dream the houses, ... 176
Oh, the sweet lies lurk in kisses! 177
Ah! those eyes again, that thrilled me, ... 178
The shades of the summer evening lie, ... 179
On paths untrodden rests the night, ... 180
Oh, death it is the cold, cold night, ... 181
Say, where is thy love, thy beauty, ... 182
The May is here with all its golden gleams, . . . 183
Into a country place the Dream-god took me, . . . 187
In the garden, 'neath the twilight, ... 192
The mother stood at the window, ... 197

FROM THE TOUR IN THE HARZ.

Coal-black dress-coats, silken stockings, ... 205
Burst, O heart, thy stony cerements! 206
On the mountain stands the cottage, ... 208
The herd-boy is a king, his throne, ... 219
See, where now the east is kindling, ... 222
I am the Princess Ilse, ... 224

MISCELLANEOUS.

Thou hast passed from life, and thou knowest it not, . . 229
Outside the blast is making riot, ... 230
The butterfly is with the rose in love, ... 232
The azure eyes of spring-time, ... 233
If thou dost but pass before me, ... 234
Oh yes ! I knew you loved me, ... 235
Strange, you say, that life, love, kisses, ... 236
With inky sails my pinnace drives, ... 237
I sit on the Runenstein and dream, ... 238
The sea is shining in the sun, ... 239
"My bachelor days that I might recall !" 240
The supercargo, Mynheer van Koek, ... 246
All under the lime-trees the music sounds, ... 254
The young Franciscan sits alone, ... 256
The night-wind through the dormers howls, . . . 257

PREFACE

TO THE THIRD EDITION OF

THE BOOK OF SONGS.

———◆———

I T is the fairy forest old,
    With lime-tree blossoms scented!
The moonshine had with its mystic light
    My soul and sense enchanted.

On, on I roamed, and, as I went,
    Sweet music o'er me rose there;
It is the nightingale,—she sings
    Of love and lovers' woes there.

She sings of love and lovers' woes,
    Hearts blest, and hearts forsaken;
So sad is her mirth, so glad her sob,
    Dreams long forgot awaken.

I

Still on I roamed, and, as I went,
　I saw before me louring
On a great wide lawn a stately pile,
　With gables peaked and towering.

Closed were its windows, everywhere
　A hush, a gloom past telling;
It seemed as though silent Death within
　These empty halls were dwelling.

A Sphinx lay there before the door,
　Half-brutish and half-human,
A lioness in trunk and claws,
　In head and breasts a woman.

A lovely woman!　The pale cheek
　Spoke of desires that wasted;
The hush'd lips curved into a smile
　That woo'd them to be tasted.

The nightingale so sweetly sang,
　I yielded to their wooing;
And as I kissed that winning face,
　I seal'd my own undoing.

The marble image thrilled with life,
　The stone began to quiver;

She drank my kisses' burning flame
With fierce convulsive shiver.

She almost drank my breath away;
And, to her passion bending,
She clasped me close, with her lion claws
My hapless body rending.

Delicious torture, rapturous pang!
The pain, the bliss, unbounded!
Her lips, their kiss was heaven to me,—
Her claws, oh, how they wounded!

The nightingale sang : "O beauteous Sphinx!
O love, love! say, why this is,
That with the anguish of death itself
Thou minglest all thy blisses?

"O beauteous Sphinx, oh answer me,
That riddle strange unloosing!
For many, many thousand years
Have I been on it musing!"

.   .   .   .

All this I might have said very well in good prose.
. . . But if one reads his old poems through again,

to give them, in view of a new edition, some polishing touches, one is somehow surprised into the old melodious habit of rhyme and cadence, and lo ! the verses, with which I introduce this third edition of " The Book of Songs." O Phœbus Apollo ! if these verses are bad, thou wilt readily forgive me. . . . For thou art an omniscient God, and thou knowest very well why I have been for so many years unable to occupy myself with metre and the clink of rhyme. . . . Thou knowest why the flame, which once enraptured the world with a brilliant display of fireworks, was suddenly diverted perforce to much more serious conflagrations. . . . Thou knowest why it is now gnawing my heart away with a silent heat. . . . Thou, O great and beauteous God, dost understand me,—thou who, upon occasion, dost exchange the golden lyre for the sturdy bow and the deadly arrows. . . . Dost thou still remember, too, that Marsyas, whom thou didst flay alive ? That was a long time back, and a similar example might be again needed. . . . Thou smilest, O mine everlasting father !

Written at Paris, the 20*th February* 1839.

HEINRICH HEINE.

YOUTH'S SORROWS

1817–1821

DREAM PICTURES.

" Mir träumte einst von wildem Liebesglüh'n."

I HAVE had dreams of wild love wildly nursed,
  Of myrtles, mignonette, and silken tresses,
 Of lips, whose blames belie the kiss that blesses,
Of dirge-like songs to dirge-like airs rehearsed.

My dreams have paled and faded long ago,
  Faded the very form they most adored,
  Nothing is left me but what once I poured
Into pathetic verse with feverish glow.

Thou, orphan'd song, art left.   Do thou, too, fade !
  Go, seek that vision'd form long lost in night,
  And say from me—if you upon it light—
With airy breath I greet that airy shade !

" Ein Traum, gar seltsam schauerlich."

A DREAM, that eerie was to see,
　　Delighted, then affrighted me.
Its gruesome sights still haunt mine eyes,
And shake my heart with wild surmise.

There was a garden wondrous fair;
Great joy had I in roaming there :
Fair flowers a-many looked at me,
Well pleased was I as man might be.

The little birds from boughs above
Piped many sprightly songs of love;
The sun was red, and rimmed with gold ;.
The flowers had bright hues manifold.

Sweet odours floated everywhere,
The breezes soft and wooing were ;
And all was lustrous, all was gay,
And wore its bravest, best array.

Within that flowery haunt, I ween,
A fountain stood of marble sheen;
And of a fair girl I was 'ware,
That washed a milk-white vestment there.

Her eyes were soft, her cheeks were sleek,
A saint-like thing, fair-hair'd and meek;
And as I gazed, oh rare to tell,
Though strange, methought I knew her well!

That rare pale maid, her task she plies,
And croons a chant in wondrous wise :
"Flow on, fountain! fountain, flow!
Wash me the linen white as snow!"

Then up to her I took my way,
And whispered low, "Oh tell me, pray,
Thou maiden all so wondrous bright,
For whom it is, this web so white?"

Then swift she spoke, "Doom follows fleet.
This web, it is thy winding-sheet."
And ere the words she well had spoke,
The whole scene faded off like smoke.

And straight by magic sleight I stood
Within a wild and darksome wood :
The trees shot up into the sky,
Bemazed and wonder-struck was I.

And hark ! A dull, dead sound, as though
An axe far off struck blow on blow !
Through bush and brake I speed apace,
And reach at length an open space.

Full in the midst, turf'd round with green,
An oak, a mighty oak, was seen ;
And lo ! that maiden weird, she hacks
And hews its trunk with whirling axe !

Stroke falls on stroke, nor stop nor stay,
She swings the axe, and croons this lay :
" Good steel sturdy, good steel fine,
Shape me, and quickly, an oaken shrine !"

Then up to her I took my way,
And whispered low, " Oh tell me, pray,
Thou maiden wondrous fair to see,
For whom this oaken shrine may be ?"

Then swift she spoke, "The hours are few :
It is thy coffin that I hew !"
And ere the words she well had spoke,
The whole scene faded off like smoke.

It stretched so far, it stretched so bare,
All waste, all barren everywhere ;
How it befell I never knew,
There I was standing all agrue.

And gazing far ahead, I note
A streak of white before me float.
I ran to it, ran, stopped, and lo !
That rare pale maid again I know.

There spade in hand, on that wide waste,
She dug the earth deep, dug with haste ;
To look at her I scarce did dare,
She was so gruesome, yet so fair.

And swiftly still her spade she plies,
And croons a chant in wondrous wise ;
"Sharp spade, stout spade, shovel and sweep,
Shovel a pit that is wide and deep !"

Then up to her I took my way,
And whispered low, "Oh tell me, pray,
Thou maiden sweet of wondrous sheen,
What may this pit thou diggest mean?"

Then swift she spoke, "Content thee !   See,
A cool grave I have dug for thee !"
And even as the words she said,
The pit she dug wide open spread.

And as I looked into the pit,
I shuddered as with an ague-fit,
And down, as smit by sudden stroke,
I tumbled headlong !—and awoke !

" Im nächt'gen Traum hab' ich mich selbst geschaut."

ONE night—'twas in a dream—myself I spied
   In black dress coat, silk waistcoat, ruffles round
  My wrists, as I were for a wedding bound;
And my love stood before me, tender-eyed.
I made a bow to her, and said, "The bride?
  Oh, I congratulate you!" Forth they wound
  These words of mine, slow, icy-chill,—a sound
As though my throat choked, and my tongue were tied.
Then all at once gushed bitter tear on tear
  From my love's eyes, and in that stormy dew
Her image sweet did wellnigh disappear.
O sweetest eyes, dear stars of love! though ye,
  Waking, oft played me false, and dreaming too,
To trust you still how ready would I be!

" Im Traum sah ich ein Männchen klein und putzig."

I SAW in dream a dapper mannikin
   That walked on stilts, each stride an ell or more ;
   White linen and a dainty dress he wore,
But it was coarse and smirched and stained within.
All inwardly was mean and poor and thin,
   Yet with a stately seeming lackered o'er ;
   His words were full of bluster, and he bore
Himself like one well used to fight and win.
"And know'st thou who he is? Come, look and guess !"
   So spake the God of Dreams, and showed me then
   Within a glass a billowy multitude.
   The mannikin before an altar stood,
My love beside him : both of them said " Yes ! "
   And countless fiends laughed loud and cried "Amen !"

" Was treibt und tobt mein tolles Blut ? "

WHAT sets my blood so mad a-spin ?
Why burns my heart with a fire within ?
My blood it boils, it foams, it seethes,
And a gnawing flame my heart enwreathes.

My blood it seethes and foams so mad,
For I an evil dream have had ;
The Son of Night came, swart and grim,
And took me away perforce with him.

He led me to a house was bright
With the blaze of torches and lamps a-light ;
There were mirth and feasting and minstrel din—
I came to the hall, I entered in.

'Twas a wedding-feast : as I came near
The guests at the table were making cheer ;
And when the bridal pair I spied,
Oh woe, my own love was the bride !

My own, own, very love was she,
The bridegroom was unknown to me ;
Close at the back of the fair bride's chair,
I took my stand in a dumb despair.

The music sounds ; I stood stock-still—
Oh the pang as the revel rose high and shrill !
The bride, she looks like a soul that's blest,
Her hands in his the bridegroom pressed !

The bridegroom fills his goblet up,
And drinks, and offers the bride the cup ;
She thanks him with a smile so frank—
Oh woe, it was my red blood she drank !

The bride a rose-cheek'd pippin took,
And gave it her groom with a sidelong look ;
He took his knife, and he cut it apart.
Oh woe, that was my very heart !

Long and fondly they ogled and eyed ;
The bridegroom boldly clasps the bride,
On her red lips kiss on kiss rains he—
Oh woe, it is cold Death kissing me !

My tongue lay in my mouth like lead,
And never a word could I have said:
High swells the music; the dance began,
And the buxom bridal pair led the van.

As I stood like one in death-trance bound,
The dancers go spinning and whirling round:
The bridegroom he whispers to the bride,—
Her cheeks flush red, but she does not chide.

" Im Süssen Traum, bei stiller Nacht."

I N sweetest dream, at dead of night,
   There came to me by wizard sleight—
By wizard sleight, my love so free,
And into my chamber she came to me.

I look at her,—oh, she was fair !
I look, and she smiles with a gentle air ;
Smiles on me till my heart swells high,
And my words gush forth with a sob and sigh.

" Take all, take all that I have, love mine—
My own, own love, it is freely thine—
So round thee I my arms may throw
From midnight on to the first cock-crow ! "

Then I felt a stound through all my frame—
So sweet, so thrilling-sad it came—
And the fair girl spoke, and her word was this,
" Oh, give to me thy hopes of bliss ! "

" My life so sweet, my youth so bright,
Will I give, and give with a fond delight,
O maiden, so angel-like, to thee ;
But my hopes of bliss—that may not be ! "

Out like a torrent my wild words flew,
But fairer, and still more fair she grew;
And ever the word she spoke was this,
" Oh, give to me thy hopes of bliss ! "

The words went booming through my brain,
And within my soul, and through every vein,
A sea of flame did seem to seethe ;
My heart grew faint, I scarce could breathe.

Then I was aware of angels white
In an aureole haze of golden light ;
But now came raging in a pack
Of goblins grizzly, and grim, and black.

With the angels they wrestled, and fought, and strove ;
Anon the angels away they drove,
And then these grim black goblins, too,
Melted in mist away from view.

I was like to swoon for joy; around
My darling fair my arms I wound;
Close as a young roe she clings to me,
But weeps the while full bitterly.

She weeps : I know well why is this,
And her rosy lips into silence kiss,—
" Oh, love mine, stifle these flowing tears;
Be mine, all mine, and have no fears ! "

" Be mine, all mine ! " Than thought more quick
My blood grows icy-cold and thick;
The earth, it crashes from side to side,
And a chasm breaks open, yawning wide.

And from that black chasm the grim black crew
Start up; pale, pale my fair love grew;
Out of my arms she vanished in air,
And all alone I was standing there.

Then round me that grim black crew begin
To dance with eldritch mow and grin;
In upon me they press and crowd,
And mocking laughter peals high and loud.

Translations from Heine.

And ever closer the circle grows,
And ever wilder the chorus rose,—
" Thou gavest thy hopes of bliss away,
And ours thou art for ever and aye !"

" Ich lag und schlief, und schlief recht mild."

I SLEPT,—my sleep was soft and sweet,
    No pain nor trouble there,—
Then did mine eyes a vision greet,
    A maid supremely fair.

Pale, pale was she as marble stone,
    And weird and strange to see;
With a light like pearls her eyes they shone,
    Her locks hung loose and free.

And slowly, slowly did she glide,
    So phantom-like and frail,
And down she lays her by my side,
    That maiden marble-pale.

Then throbs my heart like a thing possess'd,
    With passion all aglow;
But no throb stirs that fair one's breast,
    She is cold as the mountain snow.

" My breast, it neither throbs nor beats,
    It is cold as the mountain snows;
But lovè I know—its pangs, its sweets,
    And its all-mastering throes.

" My lips and cheeks bloom not with red,
    The blood in my heart is still;
But shrink not away with shuddering dread,—
    I am thine, to do thy will ! "

And madlier still she clasped me round,
    Till my very breath 'gan fail :
The cock crew ;—gone, with never a sound,
    Was the maiden marble-pale.

SONGS.

" Die du bist so schön und rein."

THOU, so fair, so pure of guile,
Maiden of the sunny smile,
Would to thee it were my fate
All my life to dedicate !

Like the moonbeams' tender shine
Gleam these gentle eyes of thine;
Thy soft cheeks so ruddy bright
Scatter rays of rosy light.

Thy dear little mouth doth show
Pearls within, a shining row;
But the gem of gems the best
Is enshrined within thy breast.

It was love divinely deep
That into my heart did leap,
When I looked on thee erewhile
Maiden of the sunny smile !

" Wenn ich bei meiner Liebsten bin."

WHEN I am with my dearest dear,
   My heart all care defies ;
Then feels my soul such wealth of cheer,
  No other wealth I prize.

But from her arms when forced to fly,
  Her fair soft arms, oh then
My riches all take wing, and I
  Am beggar-poor again.

"Morgens steh' ich auf und frage."

I AT morn get up, and "Will she
   Come," I ask, "to-day?"
I lie down at eve, and "Still she
   Cometh not!" I say.

Sleepless, restless, with heart aching,
   Night I wear away;
Dreaming, half asleep, half waking,
   Roam about by day!

" Ich wandelte unter den Baümen."

ALONE with the anguish that tore me
   'Neath the forest boughs I stept;
Anon came the old dream o'er me,
   And into my heart it crept.

Who taught ye this word, not to fear it,
   Little birds, singing up there so free?
Oh, hush ! if my heart should hear it,
   Very sad it again would be.

"This way came a fair girl, she taught it;
   As she sang, it was all we heard ;
And up we little birds caught it,
   The dainty-sweet golden word."

Never think with such fables to wile me !
   Little birds, ye are wondrously sly ;
You wish of my grief to beguile me,
   But I trust nothing living, not I.

" Lieb Liebchen, leg's Händchen auf's Herze mein."

L AY your dear little hand on my heart, my fair !
    Ah, you hear, how it knocks in its chamber
        there?
In there dwells a carpenter grim and vile,
And he's shaping a coffin for me the while.

There is knocking and hammering night and day;
Long since they have frightened my sleep away.
O carpenter, show that you know your trade,
That so to sleep I may soon be laid !

" Ich wollte, meine Lieder."

OH ! if these songs of mine were
　　But flowerets, I would twine
Them into a fragrant nosegay
　For that dearest dear of mine !

Oh ! if these songs of mine were
　But kisses for lips that pine,
I would waft them all in secret
　To rest on her cheek divine !

Oh ! if these songs of mine were
　But clusters of the vine,
I would crush out their choicest juices
　To make her a noble wine !

"Schöne Wiege meiner Leiden."

OH, fair cradle of my sorrow,
    Oh, fair tomb of peace for me,
Oh, fair town, my last good-morrow,
    Last farewell I say to thee !

Fare thee well, thou threshold holy,
    Where my lady's footsteps stir,
And that spot, still worshipped lowly,
    Where mine eyes first looked on her !

Had I but beheld thee never,
    Thee, my bosom's beauteous queen,
Wretched now, and wretched ever,
    Oh, I should not thus have been !

Touch thy heart?—I would not dare that;
    Ne'er did I thy love implore;
Might I only breathe the air that
    Thou didst breathe, I ask'd no more.

Yet I could not brook thy spurning,
  Nor thy cruel words of scorn ;
Madness in my brain is burning,
  And my heart is sick and torn.

So I go, downcast and dreary,
  With my pilgrim staff to stray,
Till I lay my head aweary
  In some cool grave far away.

" Berg' und Burgen schau'n herunter."

TOWER and castled peak look downward
  On the mirror of the Rhine,
And my bark sails blithely onward
  In the sunbeams' golden shine.

Calm I mark the ripple stealing
  O'er the broken wavelet's crest;
Silently awakes the feeling,
  Cherish'd deep within my breast.

Looking tender in its splendour
  On the stately river glides,
But the gleaming, fair in seeming,
  Death and night within it hides.

Sweet to view, at core fallacious,
  Stream, my lady's type thou art
She can wear a smile as gracious,
  Look as meek and kind of heart.

" Anfangs wollt' ich fast verzagen.

I N my lonely first despair, it
  Seemed that I could never bear it;
Yet I have borne it until now,
But do not, do not ask me how?

" Oben, wo die Sterne glühen."

W HERE above the stars are glowing,
    There the joys are surely blowing,
  Which are barred from us below :
In death's cold embraces first
Life may into warmth be nursed;
  Out of night, too, light may grow.

" Mit Rosen, Cypressen, und Flittergold."

WITH roses and cypress and tinsel gold
    Lovingly, tenderly I would enfold
This book, as though it a coffin were,
And bury my songs in their cerements there.

Could I bury my love there, I were blest !
On the grave of love grows the flower of rest;
It blooms there for all to pluck, but for me
'Twill bloom not, till laid in the grave I be.

Well, here are the songs that so wildly erst,
Like lava streams that from Ætna burst,
From the nethermost depths of my soul gush'd out,
And with lightning-flashes were freak'd about.

Now silent and corpse-like they lie, and stare
Pallid and cold, with a mist-like air;
But within them again the old fires would seethe,
If only Love's spirit should o'er them breathe.

And there come to my heart boding whispers, that say,
Love's spirit shall over them weep one day,
If ever this volume should reach thy hand,
Thou love of my soul, in a distant land.

Then the spell shall be broken that binds my lays,
The death-pale letters on thee shall gaze,—
Beseechingly gaze on thy beautiful eyes,
And breathe of love's passion, its pangs, its sighs.

ROMANCES.

THE MOUNTAIN VOICE.

A HORSEMAN rode sadly up the glen,
   A goodly knight, and brave ;
"Ah! am I bound to my true love's arms,
Or bound to the gloomy grave?"
The hill voice answer gave ;
   "The gloomy grave !"

On rode the horseman, and heavy sighs
   His soul's dismay confessed;
"And shall I then go to my grave so soon?
Be it so ! In the grave is rest !"
The voice spake this behest;
   " In the grave is rest !"

And down the horseman's cheek a tear,
   A tear of the saddest fell.;
" If in the grave there is rest for me,
Then 'twill in the grave be well !"
The voice rang like a knell ;
   " In the grave be well !"

POOR PETER.

I.

HANS and Gretel wheel and dance
　And shout, so merry their case is;
Peter stands in a corner, quite mumchance,
　And white as chalk his face is!

Hans and Gretel are bride and groom,
　And flash in their wedding gay clothes;
Poor Peter gnaws his nails in gloom,
　All in his work-a-day clothes.

And Peter, to himself says he,
　And eyes the couple sadly,
" But that I've too much sense, oh me!
　I'd end this trouble badly.

II.

" There is a pang within my breast,
　A pang that's like to break it;
And let me roam, or let me rest,
　Away I cannot shake it.

"To Gretel now it makes me hie,
    In hopes that she may cure it ;
But when I look into her eye,
    I feel I can't endure it.

"I climb up to the mountain-top,—
    There's none to hold me cheap there,—
And when I once am up I stop,
    And sit me down and weep there."

III.

Poor Peter he goes shambling by
Very slow, death-pale, and shy ;
People on the streets, they will
To look at him, poor soul! stand still.

The girls they whisper as they pass,
" Has he come from the grave, alas ? "
Ah no! ye maidens fair, I trow,
He's only going gravewards now.

His treasure he has lost, and so
'Tis the best place for him to go,
Where he his weary heart may lay,
And sleep on to the Judgment-Day.

THE PRISONER'S SONG.

"Als meine Grossmutter die Lise behext."

WHEN my grandam bewitch'd Betty Grimes, the
    folk
  Were all of a mind to burn her;
Though the judge splash'd about lots of ink, no doubt,
  To confess he could not turn her.

When into the kettle they set her a-swim,
  "Oh, murder!" she cried like a craven;
And up, as the smoke rose pitchy and grim,
  Flew off in the shape of a raven.

O black grannie mine, that art feather'd so fine,
  Come, and into my prison frisk it!
Fly in through the bars in the dull moonshine,
  And bring me some cheese and biscuit!

O black grannie mine, that art feather'd so fine,
  Contrive, if you'd save me sorrow,
That my aunt doesn't pick out these eyes of mine,
  When I swing in the wind to-morrow.

THE GRENADIERS.

FOR France two grenadiers held their way,
    Had prisoners been in Russia ;
And sorrowful men they were, when they
    The frontier reached of Prussia.

For there they heard of a dire event, —
    How the world 'gainst France had risen, her
Grande armée had shattered and shent,
    And taken her Emperor prisoner.

They mingled their tears, these two grenadiers,
    To the sad tale ever returning ;
" Oh would ! " said one, " that my days were done !
    My old wounds, how they're burning ! "

" All's up ! " said the other ; " and sooner than not
    I would die like you, never doubt me ;
But a wife and child at home I've got,
    And they must be starved without me ! "

" Hang wife and child !   It is something more,
  And better far, that I pant for ;
My Emperor prisoner !   My Emperor !
  Let them go beg what they want for !

" If I die just now, as 'tis like I may,
  Then, comrade, this boon grant me,
Take my body with you to France away,
  And in France's dear earth plant me.

" The *Croix d'Honneur*, with its crimson band,
  On my heart see that you place it ;
Then give me my rifle in my hand,
  And my sword, around me brace it.

" So will I lie, and listen all ear,
  Like a sentinel, low in my bed there,
Till the roar of the cannon some day I hear,
  And the neigh of the steeds as they tread there.

" Then I'll know 'tis my Emperor riding by ;
  Many sabres are flashing to ward him,
And out from my grave full armed spring I,
  The Emperor ! to shield and to guard him ! "

THE MESSAGE.

UP, boot and saddle, my boy! Bestride
   Your steed, and away *pêle-mêle*
To old King Duncan's castle ride
   Through forest and over fell.

Slip into the stable, and wait, till you
   Are by the groom espied,
Then ask, " Of King Duncan's daughters which,
   Now tell me, is the bride?"

And if he says, "'Tis the nut-brown girl!"
   Then speed with the tale to me;
But if he says, "'Tis the fair-hair'd maid!"
   Then slacker your speed may be.

And to the Master Twinester go,
   Buy a rope of the stoutest strand;
Ride slowly back, speak never a word,
   And lay it into my hand.

"Ich geh' nicht allein, mein feines Lieb."

I GO not alone, fair lady mine ;
  You must away with me
To the dear old vaulted chamber drear
In the sad cold house of sorrow and fear,
Where my mother cowers by the porch outside,
A-watch for her son to bring home his bride.

"Now let me go, thou gloomy man !
  What should I want with thee ?
Thy breath is hot, thine eyes flash light,
Thy hand is ice, thy cheek is white ;
But a merry life is the life for me,
'Mid roses' perfume and in sunshine free."

Let the rose waft perfume, the sun shine bright,
  Darling, my sweet, my own !
Thyself in the white flowing veil attire,
And sweep the strings of the sounding lyre,
And sing me a bridal song soft and low ;
The night wind shall pipe the tune as we go.

BELSHAZZAR.

THE midnight hour was drawing on ;
Hushed into rest lay Babylon.

All save the royal palace, where
Was the din of revel, and torches' flare.

There high within his royal hall
Belshazzar the king held festival.

His nobles around him in splendour shine,
And drain down goblets of sparkling wine.

The nobles shout, and the goblets ring ;
'Twas sweet to the heart of that stiff-neck'd king.

The cheeks of the king, they flushed with flame,
As he drank, he grew bolder, more dead to shame.

And, madden'd with pride, his lips let fall
Wild words, that blaspheme the great Lord of All.

More vaunting he grew, and his blasphemous sneers
Were hailed by his lordly rout with cheers.

Proudly the king has a mandate passed;
Away hie the slaves, and come back full fast.

Many gold vessels they bring with them,
The spoils of God's House in Jerusalem.

With impious hand the king caught up,
Filled to the brim, a sacred cup;

And down to the bottom he drain'd it dry,
And with mouth a-foam thus aloud did cry,—

"Jehovah! I scoff at Thy greatness gone.
I am the king of Babylon!"

The terrible words were ringing still,
When the king at his heart felt a secret chill.

The laughter ceased, the lords held their breath,
And all through the hall it was still as death.

And see, see there! on the white wall, see,
Comes forth what seems a man's hand to be!

And it wrote and wrote in letters of flame
On the white wall,—then vanished the way it came.

The king sat staring, he could not speak,
His knees knocked together, death-pale was his cheek.

With cold fear creeping his lords sat round,
They sat dumb-stricken, with never a sound.

The Magians came, yet not one of them all
Could read the flame-writing upon the wall.

But or ever that night did to morning wane,
Belshazzar the king by his lords was slain.

THE VOYAGE.

" Ich stand gelehnet an den Mast."

EACH wave I counted, as I stood
　　And lean'd against the mast;
Adieu, dear native land, adieu!
　　My little bark sails fast.

I pass her house, the window-panes
　　Against the sunset shine;
I look till I am almost blind,
　　But no one makes a sign!

Crowd not, ye tears, into mine eyes,
　　Still leave me power to see!
And thou, poor heart, break not with this
　　O'erwhelming agony!

ON HEARING A LADY SING AN OLD BALLAD.

" Ich denke noch der Zaubervollen,
Wie sie zuerst mein' Auge sah."

I SEE her still, that fair enchantress,
   As first my eyes upon her fell;
I hear her rich voice clear and pealing,
Into my heart's depths sweetly stealing,
Till tears relieve the quickened feeling,—
   How I was moved, I cannot tell.

Away to dreamland I was wafted;
   Methought that I was still a child;
I sit by lamplight in a nook
Of my dear mother's room, and look
In wonder on a story-book,
   While winds without are piping wild.

The stories kindle into life,
   Knights from the grave ascend anon;

There is a fight at Roncesvalles,
Sir Roland's plume towers o'er it all,
Brave falchions many attend his call,
  So, too, does caitiff Ganelon.

By him most vilely done to death,
  Bleeding and breathless Roland lies ;
Scarce could he wind the signal horn,
That to great Charles's ear was borne ;
When down he sank, foredone, forlorn,—
  And straight with him my vision dies.

Then came a crash, that from my dream
  Awoke me, a chaotic sound ;
The legend now is all told out,
The people clap their hands, and shout
" Bravo, Bravo ! " all round about :
  The singer curtseys to the ground.

A WORD TO THE WISE.

"Wenn der Frühling kommt mit dem Sonnenschein."

WHEN spring with the sunny days comes in,
    Then flowers to burgeon and bloom begin ;
When the moon has her radiant course begun,
The stars swim after her one by one ;
When a pair of sweet eyes on the poet beams,
From the depths of his soul songs gush in streams ;
But songs and stars and flowers of all dyes,
And moonbeams and sunshine and sweetest eyes,—
Be as fond of this sort of thing as you may,—
To make up a world go a very short way.

LYRICAL INTERMEZZO

1822–1823

In this volume I have set
All my anguish, all my fret ;
Open it, and thou shalt see
All my heart laid bare to thee.

'TWAS in the glorious month of May,
　　When all the buds were blowing,
I felt—ah me, how sweet it was !—
　　Love in my heart a-growing.

'Twas in the glorious month of May,
　　When all the birds were quiring,
In burning words I told her all
　　My yearning, my aspiring.　　·

" Aus meinen Thränen spriessen."

SWEET flowers spring up, the fairest,
   Where fell my tears, and burned ;
And all my sighs to melodies
   Of nightingales are turned.

And, if thou'lt love me, Sweeting,
   The flowers to thee I'll bring ;
And 'neath thy chamber window
   The nightingales shall sing.

———————

" Die Rose, die Lilie, die Taube, die Sonne !"

THE rose, the lily, the sun, and the dove,
   I loved them all with a passion of love.
That is past ; now one only is dear to me,
My pretty, my witty, pure, peerless she ;
She herself, source of all that is worthy love,
Is rose, and lily, and sun, and dove.

" Wenn ich in deine Augen seh'."

WHENE'ER I look into thine eyes,
    Then every fear that haunts me flies;
But when I kiss thy mouth, oh then
I feel a giant's strength again.

Whene'er I couch me on thy breast,
I know what heaven is to the blest;
But when thou sayest, " I love thee ! "
Then must I weep, and bitterly.

" Dein Angesicht, so lieb und schön."

THY face, so sweet and fair to see,
    Of late has come in my dreams to me ;
It is so gentle and angel-fair,
And yet so wan, so wan with care.

The lips are rose-red ; but anon
Death kisses them,—the rose is gone ;
And quench'd, alas ! the heavenly light,
That from thy sweet eyes flashes bright.

" Lehn' deine Wang' an meine Wang'."

THY cheek incline, dear love, to mine,
    Then our tears in one stream will meet, love !
Let thy heart be pressed till on mine it rest,
    Then the flames together will beat, love !

And when the stream of our tears shall light
    On that flame so fiercely burning,
And within my arms I clasp thee tight—
    I shall die with love's wild yearning.

" Ich will meine Seele tauchen."

I WILL steep my fainting spirit
   In the lily's calyx pale ;
The lily, in tones that stir it,
   A song of my love shall exhale.

That song shall vibrate and shiver,
   Like the ever-remembered kiss,
That from her lips on mine did quiver
   In an hour of divinest bliss.

" Es stehen unbeweglich."

IMMOVABLE, unchanging,
    The stars stand in the skies,
Upon each other gazing
    With sad and loving eyes.

They speak throughout the ages
    A speech so rich, so grand;
But none of all the sages
    That speech can understand.

But I that speech have mastered,
    Can all its meanings trace;
What for a grammar served me
    Was my belovèd's face.

" *Auf Flügeln des Gesanges.*"

OH, I would bear thee, my love, my bride,
  Afar on the wings of song,
To a fairy spot by the Ganges' side;
  I have known and have loved it long.

'Tis a garden a-flame with blossoms rare,
  That sleeping in moonlight lies;
The Lotus-flowers are awaiting there
  A sister they dearly prize.

There the violets twine, and soft vows repeat,
  And gaze on the stars above;
The roses exhale in whispers sweet
  Old legends of souls that love.

Gazelles come bounding from the brake,
  And pause, and look shyly round;
And the waves of the sacred river make
  A far-off slumb'rous sound.

There shall we couch by a rippling stream
  In the shade of a stately palm,
And drink in love, and delight, and dream
  Long dreams in a blissful calm.

" Die Lotosblume ängstigt."

THE lotus-flower is scared by
    The sun's resplendent beam,
And waits with head low drooping
    For night in a trancèd dream.

The moon, he is her true love,
    He wakens her with his rays,
And her sweet flower-face she fondly
    Unveils to his tender gaze.

She blushes, and flushes, and brightens,
    And looks up in silence above;
She sighs, she weeps, and she quivers
    With love, and the pangs of love.

" Du liebst mich nicht, du liebst mich nicht."

M Y love you cannot, cannot brook !
    I don't let that distress me ;
So I but on thy face may look,
    In that's enough to bless me.

You hate, you hate, you hate me ! is
    Your rosy-red mouth's greeting :
But let me have that mouth to kiss,
    And I'm content, my sweeting !

" Oh, schwöre nicht, und küsse nur !"

OH, swear not, only kiss me now.—
    I believe, not I, no woman's vow !
Thy words are sweet, but sweeter far
The kisses I've ta'en from thy sweet lips are!
Thes are mine, and in them I believe ;
Words are but vapour, and only deceive.

   .   , ...

Oh, go on swearing, sweet love of mine,
I believe thy words, just because they are thine
I swoon in rapture upon thy breast,
And believe that I am supremely blest ;
I believe thou wilt love me for ever and aye,
And after that, too,—ay, for many a day !

" Liebste, sollst mir heute sagen ? "

SAY, love, art thou not a vision,—
　　Speak, for I to know am fain—
Such as summer hours Elysian
　　Breed within the poet's brain?

Nay, a mouth of such completeness,
　　Eyes of such bewitching flame,
Girl so garner'd round with sweetness,
　　Never did a poet frame.

Vampires, basilisks, chimæras,
　　Dragons, monsters, all the dire
Creatures of the fable eras
　　Quicken in the poet's fire.

But thyself, so artful-artless,
　　Thy sweet face, thy tender eyes,
With their looks so fond, so heartless,
　　Never poet could devise.

"Wie die Wellenschaumgeborene."

FAIR she is as foam-born Venus,
    She that was my love, my pride;
But a churl has stept between us,
    Vaunts her as his chosen bride.

Heart mine, chafe not at the treason,
    O thou much-enduring one!
Bear, nay, deem it quite in reason,
    What the pretty fool has done.

" Ich grolle nicht, und wenn das Herz auch bricht."

I AM not wroth, my own lost love, although
   My heart is breaking—wroth I am not, no !
For all thou dost in diamonds blaze, no ray
Of light into thy heart's night finds its way.

I saw thee in a dream.   Oh, piteous sight !
I saw thy heart all empty, all in night ;
I saw the serpent gnawing at thy heart ;
I saw how wretched, O my love, thou art !

" Ja, du bist elend, und ich grolle nicht."

YES, thou art wretched, and I am not wroth:
   O love, in pain we both must draw our breath;
Yes, we are fated to be wretched both,
   Till our sad hearts, O love, shall break in death.

I see the scorn upon thy lips express'd,
   I see thine eye flash fierce defiance now,
I see the spasm of pride that heaves thy breast,
   Yet even as I am wretched, so art thou.

Yet round thy lips an unseen sorrow glides,
   Tears, hidden tears, bedim those eyes of thine,
Thy proud breast cherishes a wound it hides,—
   Yes, to be wretched is thy lot and mine!

" Das ist ein Flöten und Geigen."

H ARK to yon fiddling and fluting,
 The trumpets bray loudly out !
My heart's very darling is footing
 It there with her wedding rout.

Hark to yon booming and droning
 Of hautboy, bassoon, and drum !
And, mingled through all, the moaning
 And sobs of good angels come.

"So hast du ganz und gar vergessen."

AND hast thou forgotten, so fickle thou art,
  That I so long have possessed thy heart—
Thy heart so dear, and so false to me,
That nothing could dearer or falser be?

And hast thou forgotten the love, the pain,
That wildered my heart, and maddened my brain?
Which was the greater I cannot state,
I only know that they both were great.

" Und wüssten's die Blumen, die kleinen."

IF the little flowers knew how deep
   Is the wound that is in my heart,
Their tears with mine they'd weep,
   For a balm to ease its smart.

If the nightingales knew how ill
   And worn with woe I be,
They would cheerily carol and trill,
   And all to bring joy to me.

If they knew, every golden star,
   The anguish that racks me here,
They would come from their heights afar
   To speak to me words of cheer.

But none of them all can know;
   One only can tell my pain,
And she has herself—oh woe !—
   She has rent my heart in twain.

" Warum sind denn die Rosen so blass."

WHY are the roses so wan of hue,
   Oh, say to me, darling, why?
And why, love, why is the violet blue,
   In the green, green grass so shy?

The lark, why sings he so sad a chime,
   As he soars in the sky o'erhead?
Why, why exhales from the fragrant thyme
   An odour as of the dead?

Why wears the sun all the livelong day
   A look of such chill and gloom?
Oh why is the earth so ashen-gray,
   And desolate as a tomb?

And why so heart-sick and sad am I?
   Oh say, love, why this should be!
Oh say, my heart's very darling, why
   Hast thou forsaken me?

" Sie haben dir viel erzählet."

THEY told thee much, much they invented,
  The charges were many they made,
But that which my soul has tormented,
  Well, that they have never said.

They made a great fuss, and their fretful
  Complaints they envenom'd with gall;
They called me base, heartless, forgetful,
  And you lent an ear to it all.

But the very worst thing, the most mulish,
  Of that they knew nothing, not they;
Yes, the very worst thing and most foolish
  In my bosom was hidden away.

" Die Linde blühte, die Nachtigall sang."

THE linden blossomed, the nightingale sung,
  The sun was beaming with smiles of light ;
Then you kissed me, around me your arms you flung,
To your heaving bosom you clasp'd me tight.

Leaves were falling, the raven croak'd hollow and
  hoarse,
The sun was saddened, and sick with shade ;
We said " Farewell ! " like some matter of course,
And you the politest of curtseys made.

" Wir haben viel für einander gefühlt."

A MIGHTY to-do with each other we made,
     And yet we were always most proper, Heaven
          knows :
At "Husband and Wife" we have often played,
And yet we came never to words or blows.
We joked and made merry—how could we do less?—
And snatched on occasion a kiss and caress :
At last in mere babyish frolic we fell
To playing " Bo-peep" in wood and in glen,
And we've managed to play at the game so well,
That we neither can find out the other again.

" Und als ich so lange, so lange gesäumt."

AND as I linger'd so many a day
  Dreaming and roistering far away,
The time on my love's heart hung like a load,
So a wedding-robe for herself she sewed,
And for bridegroom within her soft arms she wound
The biggest young fool that might well be found.

My love, so gentle, so fair is she,
That her sweet image keeps haunting me ;
Her violet eyes, her rosy cheeks,
They glow and they bloom through the months and
    weeks.
Of all my mad follies, the maddest, I wis,
Was to let through my fingers a love like this.

" Die blauen Veilchen der Aeugelein."

THE violets blue of those eyes of thine,
    The roses red of thy cheeks divine,
The lilies white of thy hands so fine,
Bloom on and on, fresh, bright, and clear—
'Tis only your heart is dried up, my dear.

" Die Welt ist so schön, und der Himmel so blau."

THE world is so fair, and the sky so blue,
    And the breezes so soft, and so balmy, too,
And the meadow flowers are so bright of hue,
And they sparkle and gleam in the morning dew,
And all men are merry and glad to view;
Yet fain would I lie in the churchyard bed,
And nestle in close by my love that's dead.

" Mein süsses Lieb, wenn du im Grab'."

WHEN thou shalt lie, my darling, low
    In the dark grave, where they hide thee,
Then down to thee I will surely go,
   And nestle in beside thee.

Wildly I'll kiss and clasp thee there,
   Pale, cold, and silent lying;
Shout, shudder, weep in dumb despair,
   Beside my dead love dying.

The midnight calls, up rise the dead,
   And dance in airy swarms there;
We twain quit not our earthly bed,
   I lie wrapt in your arms there.

Up rise the dead; the Judgment-Day
   To bliss or anguish calls them;
We twain lie on as before we lay,
   And heed not what befalls them.

" Ein Fichtenbaum steht einsam."

A PINE-TREE stands alone on
    A bare bleak northern height;
The ice and snow they swathe it,
    As it sleeps there, all in white.

'Tis dreaming of a palm-tree,
    In a far-off Eastern land,
That mourns, alone and silent,
    On a ledge of burning sand.

————————

" Schöne, helle, goldne Sterne."

STARS, that bright and golden are,
    Greet my darling from afar;
Say I'm still the same she knew—
Sick at heart, and pale, and true.

" Ach, wenn ich nur der Schemel wär'."

(*The Head speaks.*)

OH, were I but the footstool, where
The feet of my dear lady rest,
Press how she might, I should not care,
The very pain would make me blest !

(*The Heart speaks.*)

Oh, were I but the cushion, where
She sticks her pins and needles in,
Prick how they might, I should not care,
Each prick a smile should only win !

(*The Song speaks.*)

Oh, were I but the paper roll,
From which her *papillotes* she takes,
I'd whisper to her, how my soul
For her, her only, lives and aches !

" Seit die Liebste war entfernt."

SINCE my love did me beguile
    I have quite forgot to smile ;
Stupid jokes I hear and chaff,
But I cannot, cannot laugh.

Since the day I lost her, I
Have to tears, too, said good-bye ;
Sharp my heart's pangs are and deep,
But I cannot, cannot weep.

" Philister in Sonntagsröcklein."

TOMFOOLS in their Sunday clothes ramble
 Through wood, and by meadow and dale,
They shout, and like young goats gambol,
 And the "beauties of Nature" hail.

They perceive, with owl eyes blinking,
 How romantic all round appears;
The song of the sparrows they drink in
 With very long asinine ears.

But over my chamber window
 A pall of the blackest I lay;
My ghosts upon me drop in—do
 This in the broad noonday.

She I loved in the old days appears there,
 From the region where dead souls be;
She sits down beside me in tears there,
 And my heart it is melted in me.

" Manch Bild vergessener Zeiten."

SHAPE after shape uprises
   From the grave of years long dead,
That show, when thou wert near me,
   The charmèd life I led.

By day, half dared, half dreaming,
   I rambled from street to street,—
Folk stared in amazement, a creature
   So sad and so strange to meet.

By night, oh, then it was better,
   The streets were empty and bare;
I and my shadow—none other—
   Roam'd silently everywhere.

I cross'd the bridge, and my footfall
   Re-echoed, each **step I took;**
The moon flash'd **up** from the **water,—**
   It gave me **a grave, sad look.**

In front of thy house I halted,
　And stared till mine eyes did ache,
Up, up at thy chamber window,—
　And I thought that my heart would break.

I know from thy window often
　Thou hast look'd without pang or pine,
And seen me, as there like a pillar
　I stood in the wan moonshine.

————————

" Freundschaft, Liebe, Stein der Weisen."

FRIENDSHIP, Love, the Philosopher's Stone,
　I have heard them praised, all three, I own.
I have praised them, too, and for them have sought,
But alas! alas! I have found them not.

" Ein Jüngling liebt ein Mädchen."

A YOUNG man loves a maiden,
   She somebody else prefers;
That somebody else loves another,
   Who makes him by wedlock hers.

The maiden in mere vexation,
   Because of the loss she has had,
Weds the first kind soul that offers,
   And this makes the young man mad.

'Tis an old, a very old story,
   But still it is always new;
And when and wherever it happens
   A man's heart is broken in two.

" Hör' ich das Liedchen klingen."

WHEN I hear the song, that erst
    My own heart's darling sang,
It seems that my heart must burst
    With the stress of the maddening pang.

I rush up in dark despair
    Where the crag through the forest peers;
There my anguish too hard to bear
    Finds ease for itself in tears.

" Es schauen die Blumen alle."

THE flowers all turn their gazes
    Aloft to the shining sun;
On, on to the shining ocean
    The rivers all blindly run.

Even so all my songs flutter on to
    My own shining dearest dear;
Take with you my tears and my sighs, too,
    Ye songs, sorrow-laden and drear!

" Mir träumte von einem Königskind."

I DREAMT of a monarch's daughter fair,
  And pale and sad was she ;
Clasp'd heart to heart we were sitting there,
  All under a linden-tree.

" Not for thy father's throne I pine,
  Nor his sceptre of gold I want,
I want not his crown of the diamond shine,
  'Tis for thy sweet self I pant."

" That cannot be !" to me she said ;
  " In the grave I am lying low,
And I only come to thee at dead
  Of night, for I love thee so !"

"Mein Liebchen, wir sassen beisammen."

MY love, we were sitting together
  In a skiff, thou and I alone;
'Twas night, very still was the weather,
  Still the great sea we floated on.

Fair isles in the moonlight were lying,
  Like spirits, asleep in a trance;
There strains of sweet music were sighing,
  And the mists heaved in aëry dance.

And ever more sweet the strains rose there,
  The mists flitted lightly and free;
But we floated on with our woes there,
  Forlorn on that wide, wide sea.

" Aus alten Märchen winkt es."

FROM the realm of old-world story
  There beckons a lily hand,
That calls up the sweetness, the glory,
  The sounds of a magic land.

Where huge flowers droop in the splendour
  Of closing day's golden red,
And cast on each other looks tender,
  As the looks are of lovers new wed;

Where all the trees, too, have voices,
  And all like a chorus sing,
And a sound as of music rejoices
  In the babble of every spring;

On the air songs of true love are swelling,
  Such as never elsewhere thou hast heard,
Till by yearnings divine beyond telling
  Thy soul is divinely stirred.

Oh me, if I might go thither,
   And gladden my care-worn breast,
Shake off all the sorrows that wither,
   Be happy and truly at rest !

Ah, many a time in my dreaming
   Through that region of rapture I roam !
Then the morning sun comes with its beaming,
   And scatters it all like foam.

" Ich hab' dich geliebet und liebe dich noch !"

I LOVED thee, and oh, I love thee still !
   The world to wreck may crumble,
But the flames of the love that I bear thee will
   Flash out, as the ruins tumble.

"Am leuchtenden Sommermorgen."

'TIS summer, a bright summer morning,
 And through the garden I stray;
The flowers, they prattle and whisper,
 But I not a word can say.

The flowers, they prattle and whisper,
 With pity my looks they scan;
"Oh, be not unkind to our sister,
 Thou pale-faced, woe-worn man!"

"Es leuchtet meine Liebe."

MY love in its shadowy glory
    Shines out with a lurid light,
Like a troubled and tragic story,
    That is told on a summer night.

" Lovers twain in a garden enchanted
    Alone and in silence stray ;
By the nightingales' songs they are haunted,
    And round them the moonbeams play.

" Statue-like stands the maid, uncompliant,
    On his knees at her feet is the knight ;
When on strides a brute of a giant,
    And the maiden flies off in a fright.

" The knight drops senseless and gory,
    The giant reels home to his bed——"
'Twill not be wound up, that story,
    Till the turf is laid over my head.

" Sie haben mich gequälet."

PEOPLE have teased and vex'd me,
    Worried me early and late :
Some with the love they bore me,
    Other some with their hate.

They drugg'd my glass with poison,
    They poison'd the bread I ate :
Some with the love they bore me,
    Other some with their hate.

But she, who has teased and vex'd me,
    And worried me far the most,—
She never hated me, never,
    And her love I could never boast.

" Es liegt der heisse Sommer."

'TIS summer, fiery summer
    Upon thy cheeks divine;
'Tis winter, icy winter
    In that little heart of thine.

'Twill not be so for ever,
    My own dear love that art ;
On thy cheek it will be winter,
    And summer in thy heart.

" Wenn zwei von einander scheiden."

WHEN it comes to lovers' parting,
  Each other's hands they press,
And then they fall a-weeping,
  And sigh sighs numberless.

We wept not, thou and I, love,
  Nor "Oh!" nor "Ah!" sigh'd we!
The tears and sighs came after,
  But alas! they were to be.

" Vergiftet sind meine Lieder."

MY songs, they are poison'd—poison'd !
　　How otherwise could it be?
Over the flowers of my life's fresh hours
　　Has poison been pour'd by thee.

My songs, they are poison'd—poison'd !
　　How otherwise could it be?
Many serpents I bear in my heart, and there
　　I bear with them, thee, love, thee.

" Mir träumte wieder der alte Traum."

AGAIN the old dream came back to me ;
   'Twas eve in the May-time vernal,
We sat there under the linden-tree,
   And vowed troth-plight eternal.

Oh, the vowing and vowing o'er and o'er !
   How we coo, and we fondle and bill, too !
To make me remember the vow I swore,
   You bit my hand,—with a will, too.

Oh, darling, with the eyes of light,
   Oh, darling, fair and mordant,
The vows were all as they should be, quite,
   The bite was a trifle discordant.

" Ich steh' auf des Berges Spitze."

I STAND on the mountain summit,
  And grow sentimental quite;
"Ah me, if I were a birdie!"
  I sigh forth with all my might.

Oh, if I were a swallow,
  My sweet, I would fly to thee,
And build me a little nest where
  Thy chamber windows be!

Oh, if I were a nightingale, sweet,
  I'd fly away straight to thee;
And my songs, to thee I would pipe them
  At night from the green lime-tree!

Oh, if I were a tom-noddy,
  I would fly to thy heart, for I'm sure
Thou art kind to tom-noddies,—very,—
  And ready their pangs to cure!

" Mein Wagen rollet langsam."

MY carriage rumbles slowly
    Through woodlands green and gay,
Through flowery dells, that in sunlight
    Are blossoming fresh with May.

I sit, and I muse, and dream of
    The lady I long to win,
When at the carriage-window
    Three phantom shapes look in.

They caper and make grimaces,
    So elf-like, and yet so shy;
And swirl, as mists do, together,
    And grin, and go whisking by.

" Ich hab' im Traum' geweinet."

IN dreams, oh, I have wept, love !
   I dreamed in the grave you were laid ;
I awoke, and my cheek was wet, love,
   And tears still adown it strayed.

In dreams, oh, I have wept, love !
   I dreamt you were false to me ;
I awoke, and I went on weeping
   Long, long and bitterly.

In dreams, oh, I have wept, love !
   I dreamed you still held me dear ;
I awoke, and unto this hour, love,
   Weep many a scalding tear.

" Allnächtlich im Traume seh' ich dich."

I SEE thee nightly in dreams, my sweet,
   Thine eyes the old welcome making,
And I fling me down at thy dear feet
   With the cry of a heart that is breaking.

Thou lookest at me in woful wise
   With a smile so sad and holy,
And pearly tear-drops from thine eyes
   Steal silently and slowly.

Whispering a word, thou lay'st on my hair
   A wreath with sad cypress shotten ;
I awake,—the wreath is no longer there,
   And the word I have forgotten.

" Das ist ein Brausen und Heulen."

H ARK to the roar and the howling,
    The rain, the autumnal squall !
My poor, sad darling, I wonder
    Where she is amidst it all ?

At the window I see her leaning
    In her little lonely room ;
Her eyes with tears overflowing,
    She stares out into the gloom.

" Der Herbstwind rüttelt die Bäume."

THE autumn wind rustles the tree-tops,
   The night is dark and cold;
Alone with my grey cloak round me,
   I ride across the wold.

And, as I ride, still faster
   My thoughts ride on before;
With gay light heart they bear me
   To her that I adore.

The dogs they bark, the servants
   Come out, the torches flare;
My spurs they clank and clatter,
   As I dash up the winding stair.

There is light in the carpeted chamber,
   A warm and a fragrant flush;
My darling is there to greet me,
   And into her arms I rush.

In the leaves the bleak wind rustles,
   And thus says the old oak-tree;
" Foolish horseman, a dream so foolish,
   Why should it be nursed by thee?"

" Es fällt ein Stern herunter."

A STAR is falling, falling,
From the radiant heights above ;
That star, I see it falling,
It is the star of love.

Blossoms and leaves without number
Fall from the apple-tree ;
The tricksy breezes seize them,
And toy with them fast and free.

The swan on the mere is singing,
And to and fro he steers ;
Faint grows his song and fainter,—
He sinks and he disappears.

And now 'tis so still and dreary ;
Nor leaves nor blossoms remain,
The star into atoms is shiver'd,
And hushed is the swan's sad strain.

" Der Traumgott bracht' mich in ein Riesenschloss."

THE Dream-god bore me to a giant keep,
    Where gleaming lights, and heavy weird per-
       fume,
And motley mingling crowds of men did sweep
Through winding labyrinths of room on room;
Pale crowds that hung about the doors did weep,
And wrung their hands, and cried as if for doom;
Young maids and knights stood out amid the throng,
And with the rush I too was borne along.   .

But all at once I am alone; and lo !
Passed out of view were all of human kind !
Onward I roam alone, and hurrying go
Through the still chambers, that so strangely wind.
My feet turn lead, my heart is full of woe,
An outlet almost I despair to find;
At length I reach the final door, and would
Go forth—O God ! what there before me stood ?

It was my darling at the door did stand,
On her brow sorrow, round her sweet lips pain ;
I would have turn'd, she beckons with her hand,
I wist not if in warning or disdain ;
But in her eyes a light shone, that unmann'd
And thrill'd me through and through, both heart and
    brain ;
Then, as she eyed me with a look that spoke
Sternly, yet with strange tenderness—I woke.

" Die Mitternacht war kalt und stumm."

THE midnight was cold, and still, and sad,
    I roam'd through the wood, and my heart was
    mad ;
I scared from slumber tree after tree,
And in pity they shook their heads at me.

" Am Kreuzweg ward begraben."

A T the cross-roads a wretch is buried,
 Self-slain in an evil hour ;
There is a blue flower growing,
 The Death-doomed-criminal's-flower.

At the cross-roads I stood in the silence
 And chill of the midnight hour ;
Slowly it waved in the moonlight,
 The Death-doomed-criminal's-flower.

" Wo ich bin, mich rings umdunkelt."

WHERE'ER I be, a darkness stronger
  Denser, all around me spreads,
Since thine eyes' dear light no longer
  On my path its lustre sheds.

Sweet love-stars! their golden dawning
  Never more shall glad my sight;
At my feet a chasm is yawning,—
  Sweep me hence, primeval night!

" Nacht lag auf meinen Augen."

UPON my eyes lay midnight,
   On my mouth a weight like lead;
In the churchyard I was lying,
   Stone-stiff in heart and head.

How long I had been sleeping
   Is more than I can say;
I awoke and heard a knocking,
   As there in my shroud I lay.

"Will you not get up, dear Heinrich?
   On eternity dawns the sun;
The dead have risen, and the rapture
   Of endless bliss has begun."

I cannot get up, my darling,
   I am blind as blind can be;
The light is quench'd in my eyes quite
   With the tears I have wept for thee.

" I will kiss the night, I will kiss it,
  My love, from thine eyes away ;
Thou shalt see the angels,—and see, too,
  Heaven's gladsome and grand array."

I cannot get up, my darling,
  The blood it is welling still,
Where thou to the heart didst stab me
  With a word that did more than kill.

" I will lay my hand, dear Heinrich,
  Oh, so softly upon thy heart,
And then it will bleed no longer,
  Nor know what it is to smart."

I cannot get up, my darling—
  My head, too, is bleeding, see !
I sent a bullet through it,
  The day thou wert torn from me.

" I will stanch it with my tresses—
  The wound that is in thy brain ;
And dam back the ebbing life-blood,
  And make thy head well again ! "

So soft, so sweet was the pleading,
   I could not say to it, No ;
And fain would I have uprisen,
   To my dear, dear love to go.

That moment my wounds burst open.
   And forth like a fountain broke
The blood from my head and bosom,
   And lo ! with the pang I woke !

" Die alten, bösen Lieder."

THE old, unhappy ditties,
　　The bad sad dreams long past,
'Tis now full time to entomb them,
　　So fetch me a coffin vast.

The things I will put there are many,
　　I will not as yet say what !
Even vaster must be that coffin,
　　Than Heidelberg's giant vat.

And fetch me a bier to bear it,—
　　The planks must be thick and stout ;
Also it must even be longer
　　Than the bridge Mayence brags about.

And fetch me of giants a dozen !
　　More strong they must be, I opine,
Than St Christopher in the Cathedral
　　At Cöln upon the Rhine.

The coffin they are to carry,
    And sink 'neath the ocean wave;
'Tis meet such a mighty coffin
    Be laid in a mighty grave.

Would you know why it is, this coffin,
    So vast, and so stout, and wide?
I am going to place my love in it,
    And my anguish too by its side.

THE RETURN HOME

1823–1824

ONCE upon my life's dark pathway
   Gleam'd a phantom of delight ;
Now that phantom fair has vanish'd,
   I am wholly wrapt in night.

Children in the dark, they suffer
   At their heart a spasm of fear ;
And, their inward pain to deaden,
   Sing aloud, that all may hear.

I, a madcap child, now childlike
   In the dark to sing am fain ;
If my song be not delightsome,
   It at least has eased my pain.

LORELEY.

I WIST not what it is daunts me,
  And makes me feel eerie and low :
· A legend, it troubles, it haunts me,
  A legend of long ago.

The air chills, day is declining,
  And smoothly Rhine's waters run,
And the peaks of the mountains are shining
  Aloft in the setting sun.

A maiden of wondrous seeming,
  Most beautiful, see, sits there;
Her jewels in gold are gleaming,
  She combs out her golden hair.

With a comb of red gold she parts it,
  And still as she combs it she sings;
As the melody falls on our hearts, it
  With power as of magic stings.

With a spasm the boatman hears it
  Out there in his little skiff :
He sees not the reef as he nears it,
  He only looks up to the cliff.

The waters will sweep, I am thinking,
  O'er skiff, ay, and boatman ere long ;
And this is, when daylight is sinking,
  What Loreley did with her song.

" Mein Herz, mein Herz ist traurig."

MY heart, my heart is heavy,
    Yet blithe May gladdens the land
High up 'gainst a lime-tree leaning,
    On the bastion old I stand.

Below with a tranquil motion
    The dark-blue town-moat flows;
A boy floats on in his shallop,
    And fishes and pipes as he goes.

Beyond I see, sloping upward,
    Smiling and many-hued,
Gardens, and arbours, and people,
    And cattle, and meadows, and wood.

The maidens their linen are bleaching,
    And flit on the green to and fro;
The mill-wheel shakes diamond-dust out,
    I hear its hum far below.

On the ridge of the old grey turret
　A sentinel's box I note,
And up and down stalks a soldier
　Arrayed in a red-laced coat.

He is making play with his rifle,
　It gleams in the sun's rich red ;
Arms he presents,—recovers,—
　I wish he would shoot me dead.

" Im Walde wandl' ich und weine."

I ROAM through the wood heavy-hearted,
    The throstle sits up on her bough ;
She springs and she sings very softly,—
    " What makes thee so doleful now ? "

The swallows, thy sisters, could tell thee,
    Pretty warbler up there on the tree ;
The cosy nests that they dwelt in
    Were where my love's windows be.

" Die Nacht ist feucht und stürmisch."

THE night, it is damp and stormy,
    Not a star in the sky to be seen ;
The forest-boughs creak all round me,
    I wander in silence between.

From the lonesome lodge of the huntsman
    Far flickers a feeble light ;
It shall not beguile me to it—
    On the place there's a kind of blight.

There the blind grannie's sitting, I warrant,
    In the rusty leathern chair,
Speaking never a word, like a statue
    With settled and stony stare.

To and fro strides, cursing, the forester's
    Son with the carroty pate,
Flings his rifle down in the corner,
    And laughs with the rage of hate.

The bonnie young wench is spinning,
  Fast fall her tears on the flax;
And, whimpering, close to her feet creeps
  And nestles the old man's Dachs.[1]

---

[1] The small quaint-looking dog, with a fine head and feet of the turnspit type, which is common in Thuringia and elsewhere in Germany.

" Als ich auf der Reise zufällig."

WHEN I stumbled by chance in a journey
   On my lost love's kin, the three,—
Father, mother, and little sister,—
   All smiling came up to me.

How I was and had been, they ask'd me,
   Of themselves told the self-same tale;
I was noways changed, they protested,
   Except that my face was pale.

I ask'd after aunts and cousins,
   And their friends—oh, such bores!—also;
And after the little pup-dog,
   With the bark that was soft and low.

To my old love—to her that is married—
   The talk in due time I led,
And in kindly tones they answer'd,
   She had lately been brought to bed.

And I vow'd I was quite delighted,
    And begg'd in the tenderest way
They would give her my best good wishes,
    And all sorts of kind things say.

Then in broke the little sister:
    "The pup, so gentle and fine,
Grew big and went mad, so one day
    They drown'd him, poor dear, in the Rhine!"

That child is so like my lost love,
    So like above all in her smile;
She has the same eyes, that made me
    Of men the most wretched erewhile.

" Wir sassen am Fischerhause.

WE sat by the fisherman's cottage,
 And we looked out over the Fiord ;
The evening mists spread round us,
 And upwards and upwards soared.

All at once the lights in the lighthouse
 Were lit up, and flashed out wide,
And far away in the offing
 A ship might still be descried.

We talked of tempest and shipwreck,
 · Of the sailor, and how he fares ;
How he vibrates 'twixt wind and water,
 'Twixt pleasure and toilsome cares.

We talked of far-away regions,
 Both in North and in South that were ;
Of all the singular peoples,
 And singular customs there.

There are giant woods on the Ganges,
   And sunshine and fragrant bowers,
And stately serene men kneel there
   Before the lotus flowers.

In Lapland, the natives are filthy,
   Flat-headed, broad-mouthed, and small;
They cower round their fires, and bake there
   Their fish, and jabber and squall.

The girls they listened intently,
   And at last no one spoke any more;
The ship could be sighted no longer,
   The night had sunk down on the shore.

"Du schönes Fischer-Mädchen."

MY bonnie blithe fisher-maiden,
　　Row in your boat to the strand,
And come and sit down beside me,
　　And chat with me hand in hand.

Rest your dear little head on my bosom,
　　And be not so frightened, child;
Every day you trust without thinking
　　Yourself to the ocean wild.

My heart is quite like the ocean,
　　It has tempests, and ebb, and flow;
And fine pearls lie there a-many,
　　Down, down in its depths below.

" Der Mond ist aufgegangen."

THE moon is up, and shining
    The quivering waves along ;
My love in my arms is reclining,
    Our hearts beat quick and strong.

Clasped to her breast I am lying,
    The waves lapping in to our feet ;
" Hush ! " " 'Tis but the low wind sighing !
    Why shakes so thy white hand, sweet ? "

" Ah, love, this is no wind sighing !
    'Tis the mermen's song, I know ;
And these are my sisters crying,
    Whom the sea took years ago."

" Auf den Wolken ruht der Mond."

THE moon, a giant orange, rests
　　On a bank of cloudlets tender ;
O'er the dim grey sea she sheds
　　One broad streak of golden splendour.

Down the beach I roam alone,
　　Where the waves in foam are broken ;
Many sweet words reach mine ear,
　　In the water sweetly spoken.

Oh, how slowly goes the night !
　　Speak out, heart, though speech undo me !
Nixie fair, come forth, and dance,
　　Singing fairy roundels to me !

Lay my head upon thy breast ;
　　Body, soul, I yield them wholly ;
Sing me fondly into death,
　　Kiss life from my bosom slowly!

" Eingehüllt in graue Wolken."

IN grey folds of cloud enveloped,
   Now the great gods sleep together.
Hark, their snoring! I can hear it,—
   That's what makes this stormy weather.

Stormy weather! Such mad fury
   To the poor ship bodes disaster ;
Who, ah who, these winds can bridle,
   Curb these waves that own no master?

Stop I can't the gale from raging,
   Or the masts and planks from creaking,
So I'll shroud me in my mantle,
   Like the gods, to slumber sneaking.

" Der Wind zieht seine Hosen an."

THE wild wind draws his breeches on,
    His foam-white water breeches;
The billows snore, and howl, and roar,
    As into them he pitches.

In waterspouts the rains rush down
    From black heights thunder-rended;
'Tis just as though old Night to drown
    Old Ocean's self intended.

The sea-mew to the topmast clings;
    Shrill through the tempest's raging
She screams and cries, and flaps her wings,
    Some dire mishap presaging.

" Der Sturm spielt auf zum Tanze."

THE gale tunes up for a revel,
    Pipes, whistles, and booms full sad :
Huzzah !   How the bark goes bounding !
    The night is frolic-mad.

A mountain of living water
    The sea piles up in its might ;
Here yawns an abyss, all blackness,
    There towers a battlement white.

Pukings, and prayers, and curses
    Resound up the cabin stair;
By the mast I hold on, and murmur—
    " O home, how I wish I were there !"

" Der Abend kommt gezogen."

THE twilight has died in darkness,
 The mist gathers over the sea,
The waves moan round with a mystic sound,—
 What may yonder white thing be?

The sea-nymph comes out from the breakers,
 Sits down by my side on the shore;
Her breasts of snow, they gleam and glow
 Through the filmy vest she wore.

She clasps me so close to her bosom,
 That bear it I scarcely may;
" Too tight dost thou press, too closely caress,
 Thou beautiful water-fay!"

" With clinging arms I caress thee,
 And press thee with all my might;
For in that is a charm, will make me warm
 In the chill of this bitter night."

"The moon looks paler and paler
   Through the haze of her cloudy way;
Thine eyes are more dim, and in tears they swim,
   Thou beautiful water-fay!"

"They are not more dim, nor more tearful,
   Though dim and tearful they be,
For a drop or twain within them remain,
   Which I brought with me up from the sea."

"The scream of the sea-mew is dirge-like,
   The waves climb and burst in spray,
And thy heart leaps, stirred up from its deeps,
   Thou beautiful water-fay!"

"My heart it leaps, stirred up from its deeps
   By a tempest too fierce to bind;
For I love thee too well for words to tell,
   Thou dearest of mortal kind!"

"Wenn ich an deinem Hause."

WHEN past thy house at morning
    I take my way, to see
Thy face, child, at the window,
    Is deep delight to me !

Thy dark-brown eyes seem asking,
    As my sad, pale looks they scan,
Who art thou, and what ails thee,
    Thou strange and woe-worn man?

"I am a German poet,
    Through Germany widely known;
When they name the names that are famous,
    With these they will name my own.

"And what I ail, oh many,
    Dear little one, ail the same;
When they name the worst of sorrows,
    Mine, too, they are sure to name."

"Das Meer erglänzte weit hinaus."

THE sea loomed wide, a shining flat,
    The eve its parting smile lent;
By the fisherman's lonesome house we sat,
    Alone we sat, and were silent.

Up rose the mist, the surges rose,
    The sea-mew kept round us sailing,
And tears fell thickly and fast from those
    Sweet eyes with a gentle wailing.

Upon thy hand I saw them fall,
    And there on my knees I sank down;
From thy white hand I kissed them all,
    These tears I kissed and I drank down.

Since then I have withered away,—for years
    My soul like a dead thing to me;
That ill-starred woman with her tears
    Has sent very poison through me.

"Am fernen Horizonte."

ON the verge of the far horizon
    Stands the town with steeple and tower,
And it looks like a shape of cloud-land
  In the dusk of the twilight hour.

A damp breeze ruffles the ash-grey
  Lake, as along we steer;
The beat of the boatman's oar falls
  Slow, like a dirge, and drear.

The sun flashes up for a moment,
  Just one, ere it sinks below,
And shows me the spot where I lost her,
  My darling one, years ago.

"So wandl' ich wieder den alten Weg."

SO again I am pacing the well-known streets,
  The road I so oft have taken ;
I come to the house where my darling dwelt,
  How blank it looks and forsaken !

The streets are too narrow, they shut me in !
  The very stones of them scare me !
The houses fall on my head ! I fly
  As fast as my feet can bear me !

———

" Ich trat in jene Hallen."

INTO yon halls I stept,
  Where she with her troth-plight bound me ;
Where once her tears were wept,
  Are serpents crawling round me.

" Still ist die Nacht, es ruh'n die Gassen."

STILL is the night, and the streets are lone,
  My darling dwelt in this house of yore ;
'Tis years since she from the city has flown,
  Yet the house stands there as it did before.

There, too, stands a man, and aloft stares he,
  And for stress of anguish he wrings his hands ;
My blood runs cold when his face I see,
  'Tis my own very self in the moonlight stands.

Thou double ! Thou fetch, with the livid face !
  Why dost thou mimic my love-lorn mould,
That was racked and rent in this very place
  So many a night in the times of old ?

" Wie kannst du ruhig schlafen ?"

SLEEP, and in peace?   How canst thou?
    And know I am still alive?
Back comes the old wrath, and straightway
    My yoke in sunder I rive.

Dost know the old-world legend,
    How once a youth that was dead
At midnight drew his sweetheart
    Down, down to his churchyard bed?

Oh trust me, thou gracious wonder,
    Thou beauty, too fair to see !
I live, yes, live, and am stronger,
    Than legions of dead men be !

" Die Jungfrau schläft in der Kammer."

THE girl is asleep in her chamber,
   The moon looks quivering in ;
Outside there is humming and strumming,
   As of tunes when the waltzers spin.

" I will look out and see from my window,
   Who troubles my rest down below."
And there stands a skeleton fiddling,
   And he sings, as he jerks his bow :

" Once you promised to dance as my partner,
   You broke your word ; and to-day
There's a ball going on in the churchyard,
   We'll dance it out there, come away ! "

The voice strikes home to the maiden,
   It wiles her out at the door ;
She follows, as singing and fiddling,
   The skeleton strides on before.

It fiddles, and skips, and cuts capers,
   Clap, clap ! go its bones, and its skull
Keeps gruesomely nodding and nodding
   In the eerie moonshine dull.

" Ich stand in dunkeln Träumen."

I STOOD on her picture gazing,
  And backward my dark dreams ran,
And the dear, dear face before me
  To live somehow began.

Her lips, around them gathered
  A smile in some wondrous wise,
And tears as of yearning sadness
  Stood glistening in her eyes.

And down my cheeks the tears, too,
  Flowed on in unbidden stream ;
And oh, that I've lost thee, darling,
  Seems only a wildered dream !

" Ich unglücksel'ger Atlas ! Eine Welt."

I A most ill-starr'd Atlas ! I am doom'd
    To bear a world, all the whole world of sorrow ;
To bear what is not bearable, and suffer
A slow heart-breaking anguish.

Thou haughty heart, thou hast e'en will'd it so !
Thou wouldst be happy, infinitely happy,
Or infinitely wretched, haughty heart,
And see now, thou art wretched !

" Die Jahre kommen und gehen."

YEARS come and go; generations
    Are perishing day by day,
But the love that my heart aches with,
    It never will pass away.

If once, but once, I might see thee,
    And sink on my knees at thy feet,
And, dying there, dying might tell thee,
    " I love thee, I love thee, sweet ! "

" Mir träumte : traurig schaute der Mond."

I HAD a dream ; the moon looked drear,
  And drearly the stars shone o'er me ;
Away to the city, where dwells my dear,
  Many hundred miles it bore me.

It led me on to her home : I kissed
  The stones of the stair at the door there,
Which often her tiny foot had pressed,
  And the hem of her robe swept o'er there.

The night was long, the night was chill,
  The chill of the stones, it shocked me ;
And a death-pale form at the window-sill,
  Lit up by the moonshine, mocked me.

" Was will die einsame Thräne ?"

WHAT'S this?   A tear, one only?
　　It blurs and troubles my gaze.
In my eye it has hung and lingered,
　A relic of olden days.

It had many shining sisters,
　But away they all have passed—
Passed with my torments and raptures
　In night on the driving blast.

Away, too, have passed like a vapour
　Those deep-blue starlets twain,
That smiled those raptures and torments
　Right into my heart and brain.

Like a breath my very love, too,
　Has faded and flown, alas !
So now, old, lonely tear-drop,
　'Tis time thou too shouldst pass !

" Der bleiche, herbstliche Halbmond."

THE waning autumn moon looks
 Through clouds that are o'er it blown;
The pastor's house, by the churchyard,
 Stands silent and alone.

The mother is reading the Bible,
 Staring into the lamp is the son;
One daughter sleepily stretches
 Herself; says the younger one:

" How drearily, drearily follows
 One day on another, ah me!
'Tis only when some one is buried,
 There's anything here to see."

Says the mother, as she sits reading:
 " You're wrong; only four have died
Since the day they buried your father
 By the lych-gate there outside."

Says the elder daughter, yawning:
   " I won't go on starving with you;
I'll be off to the Count to-morrow,
   He's rich, and he loves me too ! "

" At the Crown are three jolly fellows,"
   Cries the son, with a laugh, "and they
Know how to make gold by the handful,—
   They'll readily teach me the way ! "

The mother she flings the Bible
   Full into his haggard face;
" So you mean to turn robber, accursèd
   Of God and of all your race ! "

They hear a knock at the window,
   They are 'ware of a beckoning hand;
Outside they see the dead father
   In his preacher's black cassock stand.

"Das ist ein schlechtes Wetter."

'TIS the very roughest of weather,
    Rain and tempest and sleet;
I sit in the dark at my window,
    And look down the desolate street.

And slowly along it wending,
    I see one lonesome ray;
'Tis a poor old soul of a mother,
    With a lanthorn groping her way.

To buy flour, eggs, and butter,
    I am certain, thus out she stirs;
She wants to make something dainty
    For that great big daughter of hers,

Who lounges at home in the arm-chair,
    And blinks at the lamp apace,
With her golden ringlets tumbled
    All over her buxom face.

" Man glaubt, dass ich mich gräme."

PEOPLE think, for love I am wasting,
    That my heart is wellnigh broke;
And I've come myself to believe it
    As firmly as other folk.

Thou great-eyed dear little creature,
    I have vow'd to thee day after day,
That words cannot tell how I love thee,
    That love gnaws my heart away.

But 'tis only alone in my chamber
    These passionate speeches have come;
And, alas! when I had thee before me,
    I have always been utterly dumb.

Oh yes, there were wicked spirits,
    Who sealed up my lips then and there;
And 'tis all through their wicked misdoings,
    That now I am sunk in despair.

" Deine weissen Lilienfinger."

OH, if thy white lily fingers
 I but once again might kiss,
Press them to my heart, and swooning,
 Fade away in speechless bliss !

Thy clear violet eyes before me
 Flit all day and night, I ween ;
And one question still torments me,
 "What may these sweet riddles mean ?"

" Hat sie sich denn nie geäussert ?"

HAS she never, then, given token
  How she takes your vows and sighs?
Could you never read requital
  Of your passion in her eyes?

Through her eyes, friend, could you never
  To her soul an entrance find?
Yet you never were a noodle
  In affairs of such a kind.

" Sie liebten sich Beide, doch Keiner."

THEY both were in love, but neither
    The heart's sad secret told ;
They were wasting away with love's fever,
    But their looks were distant and cold.

At length they were parted, and only
    In dreams now and then they met ;
They had long been dead, these lovers,
    But scarce were aware of it yet.

———

" Und als ich euch meine Schmerzen geklagt."

WHEN I told you my troubles, my tale of despair
    You received with a yawn and a silent stare ;
But when I arrayed it in dainty rhyme,
Oh, then you pronounced me superb, sublime !

" Mein Kind, wir waren Kinder."

MY bairn, we aince were bairnies,
　　Wee gamesome bairnies twa;
We creepit into the hen-house,
　　An' jookit under the straw.

We craw'd like the cock-a-doodles,
　　An' to hear us the passing folk
At ilk "kickeriki" wad fancy,
　　It just was the bantam cock.

The kists in the yaird we papered,
　　And made them bonnie and crouse,
An' we dwalt there, we twa thegither—
　　The laird had nae brawer house!

An' aften the neebor's auld baudrons
　　Look'd in for a mornin' ca',
We made her our bobs and curtsies,
　　And snoovelin' speeches an' a'.

" An' how hae ye been ? an' how are ye ? "
  Was aye the o'erword when she came ;
To mony a queer auld tabby
  Sin' syne hae we said the same.

Whiles, like auld carles we sat, too,
  And oh ! what gran' sense we talk'd then :
An' bemoan'd us, how things were a' better
  In times when oursels were young men.

How love, an' leal hearts, an' devout anes
  Had flown frae the warld clean awa',
How the price coffee stood at was awfu',
  An' gowd no to come by ava'.

They are gane, thae ploys o' my childhood,
  An' a' things are ganging, guid sooth,
The gowd, time itsel', and the warld,
  Love, faith, and leal-hearted truth.

" Das Herz ist mir bedrückt und sehnlich."

M Y heart is sad, with sore misgiving
    I think of days of " auld lang syne ; "
The world was pleasant then to live in,
    And folks were neither fast nor fine.

But everything is out of gear now,
    Such push and struggle, care and dread ;
Of God on high we have no fear now,
    And down below the devil's dead.

And things look crumbling all to ruin,
    So bleak, so dismal ; were it not
For here some billing, there some cooing,
    What would there be to live for—what ?

" Wie der Mond sich leuchtend dränget."

AS the moon through clouds that darkle
    Flashes forth with sudden light,
So through darkling memories rises
  On my soul a vision bright.

On the deck we all are seated,
  Gaily down the Rhine we go,
And the meadows, green with summer,
  In the evening sunshine glow.

At a lady's feet I laid me,
  Fair she was and full of grace;
Rosy golden gleams of sunshine
  Played upon her sweet pale face.

Oh, how gay we were, how happy!
  Lute and voice made music rare;
Bluer grew the sky, the spirit
  Seemed as it were winged on air.

Hill and castle, wood and meadow,
  Swept along in faery wise;
And the whole scene, I beheld it
  Mirror'd in that lady's eyes.

"Im Traum sah ich die Geliebte."

IN a dream I saw my darling,
   A woman all woe-begone,
She, that was once so blooming,
   Faded and shrunken and wan :

One child in her arms she carried,
   And one by the hand she leads;
Want and sore trouble are seen in
   Her look and her gait and weeds.

Through the market-square she tottered,
   And there she crosses my way,
And she looks at me, and calmly
   And sadly to her I say:

" Come to my home, come with me,
   Thou art pale and weak and ill;
I will work all day to find thee
   Both food and drink, I will.

"And I will cherish and guard, too,
  The children are with thee there;
But thyself, poor luckless darling,
  Shall be, above all, my care.

"No word shall ever escape me
  Of my love long cherished and deep;
And when thy sorrows are ended,
  I'll lie on thy grave and weep."

" Herz, mein Herz, sei nicht beklommen."

HEART, heart mine, no longer vex thee,
  But thy weird in patience dree;
Soon returning Spring will bring thee
  What the winter took from thee.

Think, how much, how much is left the
  How the world is still so fair!
And, heart mine, whate'er delights thee,
  Thou to love mayst freely dare!

" Du bist wie eine Blume."

THOU art even as a flower is,
    So gentle, and pure, and fair ;
I gaze on thee, and sadness
    Comes over my heart unaware.

I feel as though I should lay, sweet,
    My hands on thy head, with a prayer
That God may keep thee alway, sweet,
    As gentle, and pure, and fair !

"Kind! es wäre dein Verderben."

CHILD! it would be your undoing;
   And I struggle hard, you see,
That your dear kind heart may never
   Feel the glow of love for me.

That too well I have succeeded,
   Pains me in my own despite;
And I often think, "Oh, would you
   Love me, come whatever might!"

" Wenn ich auf dem Lager liege."

WHEN abed I lie enfolded
 In pillows and in night,
A form, all grace and sweetness,
 Floats ever in my sight.

Even as mine eyes are closing
 In the caress of sleep,
That dear, dear form serenely
 Into my dreams doth creep.

Yet with the dreams of morning
 It will no more depart,
For all day long I bear it
 About me in my heart.

" Mädchen mit dem rothen Mündchen."

L ASSIE with the lips sae rosy,
   With the eyne sae saft and bricht,
Dear wee lassie, I keep thinkin',
   Thinkin' on thee day and nicht.

Winter nichts are lang and eerie;
   Oh, gin I were with thee, dear,
Arms about thee, cracking couthly,
   With nae mortal by to hear!

With my kisses I would smother
   Thy white hand sae jimp and sma',
And my tears for very rapture
   On that wee white hand should fa'.

"Mag da draussen Schnee sich thürmen."

FATHOMS deep may drift the snow,
   It may hail, and it may blow,
Till my windows groan and shake,
Moan for that I ne'er will make,
For, while in my breast I bear
My love's image, spring is there.

" Verrieth mein blasses Angesicht."

WHAT I suffer for love can you
   Not read in my wan worn face?
Would you have my proud lips sue,
  Like a beggar, for alms of grace?

Oh, my lips are too proud by far,
  They can kiss and jest—that's all ;
Though for grief I were dying, they might
  Very likely drop words of gall.

" Ich wollte bei dir weilen."

I WANTED to linger about you,
  To sit by your side, but you
Were bent upon turning me out, you
  Had such a deal to do.

My soul—this I vowed with much feeling—
  To you and you only was bound;
You laughed—your laugh shook the ceiling—
  And made me a curtsey profound.

Still you went on tormenting and trying
  My passion, but, worse than all this,
You wound matters up by denying
  Me even the parting kiss.

Though you treat me even worse, do not fancy,
  I'll blow out my brains—no, no!
You are not the first, mistress Nancy,
  By many, has used me so!

"Saphire sind die Augen dein."

YES! sapphires are those eyes of thine,
    Those eyes so fond and sweet:
Oh me! thrice happy is the man,
  Whom they with love shall greet!

Thy heart, it is a diamond, shoots
  All noble lights by turns:
Oh me! thrice happy is the man,
  For whom with love it burns!

True rubies are those lips of thine,
  None finer e'er were known:
Oh me! thrice happy is the man,
  To whom their love they own!

But let me catch that happy man
  Alone in some green glade,
And of his happiness and him
  Short work shall soon be made!

" Ich hab' mir lang den Kopf zerbrochen."

I HAVE racked my brain this many a day,
   Thinking and brooding upon the past;
But the lights in thy darling eyes that play
   Have settled my wavering soul at last.

Where beam thine eyes, love, I remain,
   Fixed by their lustre so sweet, so sage,—
That I should ever have loved again,
   I could not have dreamed, though I lived an age.

" Sie haben heut' Abend Gesellschaft."

THEY have company coming this evening,
  And the house is ablaze with light;
Up yonder a figure in shadow
  Sweeps past by the windows bright.

Thou seest me not,—in the darkness
  I stand here, under thy room;
Still less canst thou see the darkness
  Is shrouding my heart in gloom.

My dark heart loves thee, adores thee,
  It loves, and it breaks for thee,
Breaks, quivers, wells out its dear life-blood,
  But all this thou dost not see!

" Ich wollt', meine Schmerzen ergössen."

OH, would all the anguish I suffer
   Might into one word be pent!
To the wayward winds I would give it,
   To carry wherever they went.

That word, brimming over with anguish,
   To thee, O my love, they should bear;
Thou shouldst hear it every moment,
   Thou shouldst hear it everywhere.

When thine eyes were closing in slumber,
   'Twould be there like a spell supreme
And that word of mine should pursue thee
   Even into thy deepest dream!

" Du hast Diamanten und Perlen."

PEARLS hast thou and diamonds, dearest,
   Thou hast all that men hold in store,
And eyes, never maiden had finer,—
   Sweet, what dost thou wish for more?

To those wonderful eyes of thine, sweet,
   Whole torrents of song I pour,
That shall make their renown immortal,—
   Sweet, what dost thou wish for more?

With those wonderful eyes thou hast made me
   Ache to my very heart's core,
Yes, won and completely undone me,—
   Sweet, what dost thou wish for more?

" Ich hab' euch im besten Juli verlassen."

JULY was quite at its best when I left you,
    I find you in January once more;
Then you sat in the sunshine stewing,
    Now you're cooled down, nay, chilled to the core.

I am off again soon, and again should I ever
    Return, you will neither be hot nor cold ;
Over your grave I shall then be treading,
    My own heart shrivelled and shrunk and old.

" Wir fuhren allein im dunkeln."

ALONE through the dark we travelled
   All night in the mail, and we
Were somehow drawn closely together,
  And merry as well could be.

But when morning broke, we were startled,
  For then we became aware,
That Love had been travelling with us,
  Without having paid his fare.

" Wie dunkle Träume stehen."

LIKE ghosts in a dream the houses
　　Stretch out in a lengthen'd row;
My mantle wrapt closely round me,
　　Before them in silence I go.

The belfry of the cathedral
　　Proclaims midnight; and now
With her charms and her kisses my darling
　　Is waiting for me, I trow.

The moon companions my footsteps,
　　Shines kindly on me as I go;
I am here at the house, and upwards
　　These words in my joy I throw:

" I thank you, dear friend, for the brightness
　　You over my path have shined;
You have my full leave to be going,
　　Now illumine the rest of mankind!

" And if you shall light on a lover,
　　Lamenting his pain alone,
Console him, as you have consoled me
　　In the sad, sad times that are flown."

" In den Küssen welche Lüge."

OH, the sweet lies lurk in kisses !
   Oh, the charm of make-believe !
Oh, to be deceived sweet bliss is,
   Bliss still sweeter to deceive !

What thou'lt grant, I know, my fairest,
   Vowing, " Nay, I never must ! "
I will trust whate'er thou swearest,
   I will swear what thou wilt trust.

" Ach, die Augen sind es wieder."

AH ! those eyes again, that thrilled me
    Once, and brightened all my going ;
And those lips, that once with sweetness
    Filled my life to overflowing !

And that voice, too !   But to hear it,
    Once my very soul has faltered !
They are still the same I left them—
    I, the wanderer, I am altered.

With her fair white arms around me
    Clasped in passionate devotion,
Now against my heart I hold her,
    Cold and dead to all emotion.

" Dämmernd liegt der Sommerabend."

THE shades of the summer evening lie
    On forest and meadows green ;
The golden moon shines in the azure sky
    Through balm-breathing air serene.

The cricket is chirping the brooklet near,
    In the water a something stirs,
And the wanderer can in the stillness hear
    A plash and a sigh through the furze.

There all by herself the fairy bright
    Is bathing within the stream ;
Her arms and throat, bewitching and white,
    In the moonshine glance and gleam.

" Nacht liegt auf den fremden Wegen."

ON paths untrodden rests the night,
   On aching heart and limbs aweary ;—
Ah, down, sweet moon, thy gentle light
  Flows like a blessing calm and cheery !

Sweet moon, thou with thy rays dost scare
  Night's terrors that were round me growing ;
My sorrows seem to melt in air,
  And tears mine eyes are overflowing.

" Der Tod das ist die kühle Nacht."

OH, death it is the cold, cold night,
    And life it is the sultry day;
'Tis growing dusk, I am drowsy—
The long, long day has tired me quite.

Over my bed there arches a tree;
There sings the early nightingale—
She sings of love all the livelong night;
Her song comes even in my dreams to me.

" Sag', wo ist dein schönes Liebchen ? "

SAY, where is thy love, thy beauty
    Whom thou sang'st of once so sweetly
When love's flames with force of magic
    Overran thy heart completely?

Ah, these flames are all extinguish'd !
    And my heart is drear and cold ;
And this little book the urn is,
    That doth my love's ashes hold.

THE TWILIGHT OF THE GODS.

THE May is here with all its golden gleams,
    Its silky breezes, and its spicy odours;
Kindly it beckons with its snowy blooms,
Greets us from countless azure violet eyes,
Spreads a green carpet out, begemm'd with flowers,
Dappled with sunshine and with morning dew,
And calls on earth's dear sons to come abroad.
To her first call they, simple folk, give ear.
The men put on their breeches of nankin,
And Sunday coats, with buttons golden-bright;
In innocent white the women robe themselves;
The young men trim mustachios still in bud;
The girls allow their bosoms fuller play;
The poets of the town their pockets fill
With paper, pencil, and field-glass : and so
The giddy throng make for the gate with shouts,
And camp outside upon the verdant grass,
Marvel how busily the trees do grow,
Play with the delicate many-tinted flowers,

List to the carols of the sportive birds,
And shout aloft to the blue vault of heaven.
  The May came to me also. At my door
Thrice did she knock and cry, " I am the May !
Thou pale-faced dreamer, I will kiss thee ! Come ! "
I kept my door close bolted, and cried out :
" In vain thou lurest me, thou ill-starr'd guest ;
I have seen through thee, ay, seen through and through
The fabric of the world, have seen too much,
And far too deeply,—all my joy is flown,
And ceaseless pangs have seized upon my heart.
I look right through the hard and stony husks
Of human houses and of human hearts,
And see in both lies, and deceit and woe.
Upon men's faces I can read their thoughts—
Bad, many. In the maiden's blush of shame
I see the throbbing of concealed desire ;
Upon the young enthusiast's haughty head
I see the motley jester's cap and bells ;
And on the earth I see but shapes grotesque
And sickly phantoms, and I know not if
It be a madhouse or an hospital.
I look down to the base of the old earth,
As though it were of crystal, and I see
The ghastly things that with her gladsome green
May vainly strives to hide. I see the dead ;
Penn'd in their narrow coffins low they lie

With folded hands, with vacant staring eyes,
And through their lips the yellow blind-worms crawl.
I see the son, his paramour with him,
Sit down for pastime on his father's grave;
The nightingales sing mocking songs around;
The gentle meadow-flowers grin bitter scorn;
Within his grave the sleeping father stirs,
And spasms of pain convulse old mother earth.
　Thou hapless earth, thy miseries I know!
I see the fever raging in thy breast;
I see thee bleeding from a thousand veins;
I see thy wounds, how they burst wide agape,
And from them flames gush out, and smoke, and blood.
I see thy all-defying giant sons,
Primeval brood, from dusky chasms ascending,
And swinging flaming torches in their hands.
They fix their iron ladders, and dash up
Madly to storm the citadel of heaven;
And swarthy dwarfs climb after them, and all
The golden stars above crash into dust.
With reckless hands they tear the golden curtain
From God's own tent; the angel hosts fall down
Upon their faces with a piercing cry;
Upon his throne God sits, pale, ashy pale,
Plucks from his head the diadem, tears his hair;
Near and more near the rabble rout sweeps on;
The giants hurl their blazing brands afar

Through the vast firmament; the dwarfs with thongs
Of quick flame scourge the angels, where they lie,
Who writhe and cower in agonies of pain,
And by the hair are dragg'd perforce away :
And mine own angel 'mongst the rest I see,
With his fair locks, and gracious lineaments,
With love that cannot die about his lips,
And in his azure eyes the calm of bliss ;—
And a black goblin, hideous to the sight,
Snatches him up, that angel pale of mine,
Eyes over with a grin his noble limbs,
Clutches him tight with a caressing gripe—
Then rings a wild shriek through the universe ;
The pillars topple, earth and heaven collapse,
And ancient Night resumes her ghastly reign.

RATCLIFF.

INTO a country place the Dream-god took me,
   Where weeping-willows waved a welcome to me
With their long verdant arms, and where the flowers
With sisterly sage eyes look'd calmly at me ;
Where the birds twittered fearlessly around me,
Where even the dogs' bark seem'd well known to me,
And moving shapes and voices greeted me
As a familiar friend, and yet where all
Struck me as strange, so weirdly, wildly strange !
Within my breast was tumult, in my head
A perfect calm ; and calmly I shook off
The dust of travel from my clothes ; the bell
Rang shrilly, and the door flew open wide

   Within were men and women, many old
Familiar faces.   A mute sorrow lay
On all, and secret shrinking pain.   With looks
Strangely confused and piteous did they eye me,
Whereon a shuddering fear ran through my soul,
Prophetic of disaster yet unknown.

Anon I recognised old Margaret.
I fix'd my eyes upon her, but she spoke not.
"Where is Maria?" I said ; and still she spoke not,
But took me gently by the hand and led me
Through a long range of chambers brightly lit,
Where wealth and pomp and deathlike silence reign'd.
At last she led me to a darken'd room,
And pointed, with averted face the while,
To a figure seated on a sofa there.
"Are you Maria?" I inquired.   I felt
An inward wonder at the gaiety
With which I spoke.   Metallic, stony hard
A voice resounded, "So the people call me !"

   On this a cutting pang pierced me like ice,
For that cavernous chilly sound was yet
Maria's voice which was so sweet of yore,—
That woman in the faded lilac dress,
Flung loosely on, with bosom all unbraced,
Her eyes set in a glassy stare, the muscles
Of her pale cheeks relax'd and leather-like,—
Ah me ! that woman was Maria, once
So bright, so fair, so framed to kindle love !
"You have been long upon the road ?" she cried,
In an uncanny, strange, familiar way.
"You look no longer delicate, dear friend ;
You are well, and sturdiness in thigh and calf
Betokens solid health !"   A winning smile

Trembled about the pallid saffron lips.
In my confusion the words blurted out
"They told me you were married!" "Yes, oh yes!"
Her voice was loud and reckless, and she smiled;
" I have a wooden stick, that is encased
In leather, calls me spouse; still, wood is wood!"
And then she laugh'd a grating toneless laugh,
That sent a chilling anguish through my soul,
And there came over me the doubt,—Are these
Maria's lips, the pure, the flowerlike-pure?
But, as she spoke, she rose, caught quickly up
A cashmere from the sofa, threw it round
Her shoulders, put her arm in mine, and so
Led me away, pass'd through the open house-door,
And took me on through field and wood and glade.
  The sun's red disk, a ball of fire, was low
Within the heavens, its purple blazed across
The trees, the flowers, the meadows, and the stream,
That in the distance flow'd majestical.
" Dost see the mighty golden eye that gleams
In the blue ether?" suddenly she cried.
" Hush, thou poor soul!" I said, and on me grew
A fairy vision in the fading light.
Out of the meadows misty shapes arose,
With white thin arms about each other twined.
The violets eyed each other tenderly;
Fondly the lily bells bent each to each,

On all the roses passionate ardours glow'd,
And the carnations breathed out burning breath;
In wealth of fragrance revell'd all the flowers,
And all wept tears of silent ecstasy,
And with one voice they sigh'd forth, " Love, Love,
    Love !"
The butterfly flashed to and fro, the bright
Anemones their fairy carols humm'd,
The evening breezes whisper'd, the oaks rustled,
The nightingale sang silver-toned and clear;
And amid all the whispering, rustling, singing,
Prattled with cold metallic tuneless voice
The faded she, that hung upon my arm.
" I know their doings at the castle nightly:
Yonder long phantom is a good kind soul,
He nods and becks to everything one wants;
The blue-coat is an angel; but the red,
With the bare sword, he is your deadly foe;"
And much else that was odd and marvellous
She went on prattling, and at length, tired out,
She sat down with me on a mossy bank,
That spread its velvet 'neath the aged oaks.

So sat we there together, still and sad,
Gazed each on each, and ever sadder grew.
The oak moan'd as with sighs of dying men;
The nightingales sang threnodies o'erhead;
Still through the leaves a red light made its way;

It play'd around Maria's pallid face,
And drew out fire from her set staring eyes;
And with the sweet voice of old times she said,
"How didst thou know, I am so wretched? I
Read of it lately in thy frenzied songs." [1]
    A chill like ice went through my breast,—I shudder'd
At my own mad impatience to behold
The future,—darkness settled on my brain,
And out of very horror I awoke.

[1] See the poems pp. 66 and 67 *ante.*

DONNÁ CLARA.

I N the garden, 'neath the twilight,
   The Alcaidè's daughter wanders;
Drum and trump send festal music
Downwards from the castle ramparts.

" Tedious are to me the dances,
And the honeyed words that flatter,
And the knights who, debonairly,
With the sun himself compare me.

" Everything is doubly tedious,
Since I saw, beneath the moonlight,
Yonder knight, who to my casement
With his lute o' nights has lured me.

" Oh, how brave he looked, and slender!
And his eyes shot piercing splendours
From his face so nobly pallid.
Truly he St George resembled !"

In this wise mused Donna Clara;
On the ground her eyes were poring;
Looking up, there stands the comely
Unknown Paladin before her.

Hand-locked, murmuring loving whispers,
In the moonlight they go dreaming;
And the zephyr fans them softly,
Fairy-like the roses greet them.

Fairy-like the roses greet them,
Like Love's heralds, all a-glowing.
" Tell me wherefore, love, thou turnest
All at once so flushed and rosy?"

"'Twas a gnat that stung me, dearest;
And these gnats in summer weather
Are to me as odious, as though
They were long-nosed Hebrew vermin."

"Think not, sweet, of gnats or Hebrews!"
Says the knight, in accents fondling.
"From the chestnut-trees in thousands
Flakes of snow-white blooms are falling.

" Flakes of snow-white blooms in thousands
Breathe around delicious odours.
Ah ! my own belovèd, tell me,
Is thy heart mine, all mine, only?"

" Yes, I love thee.   O my darling,
By the Saviour blest I swear it,
Whom the Jews, of heaven accursèd,
In their malice murdered basely !"

" Name not Saviour ! name not Hebrews !
Says the knight, in accents wooing,
" Yonder like a dream, are waving
Milk-white lilies bathed in moonshine.

" Milk-white lilies, bathed in moonshine,
On the stars aloft are brooding:
Ah ! my own belovèd, tell me,
Hast thou, too, not sworn untruly?"

" Untruth is not in me, dearest,
As within me there can be not
One small drop of blood of Moor, nor
Of that filthy race of Hebrews !"

" Think not, sweet, of Moor or Hebrew ! "
Says the knight, in tones caressing ;
And he leads the Alcaidè's daughter
Onwards to a grove of myrtles.

Stealthily love's silken meshes
He has round and round her woven !
Few the words and long the kisses,
And their hearts are overflowing.

Sings the nightingale, low-fluting,
As 'twere some bride-song ecstatic ;
And along the ground the glow-worms
As in mazy torch-dance scatter.

In the grove the hush grows deeper;
Nought is heard save through the silence
Prudent myrtles, lowly lisping,
And the flowers their fragance sighing.

Of a sudden from the castle
Comes the blare of drum and clarion ;
And, awaking, Donna Clara
Steals from the embrace that clasps her.

" Hark ! they call me, O my darling !
But thou shalt, before we sever,
Tell me thy dear name, by thee, love,
Kept so long from me a secret."

And the lover, smiling gaily,
Kissed the fingers of his Donna—
Kissed her lips, and eyes, and forehead,
And her thus at length accosted :

" I, Señora, your belovèd,
Am the son of the high-honour'd,
Far-famed, and most learned Rabbi,
Israel of Saragossa."

THE PILGRIMAGE TO KEVLAAR.

I.

THE mother stood at the window;
Her son lay in bed, alas!
"Will you not get up, dear William,
To see the procession pass?"

"O mother, I am so ailing,
I neither can hear nor see;
I think of my poor dead Gretchen,
And my heart grows faint in me."

"Get up, we will go to Kevlaar;
Your book and rosary take;
The Mother of God will heal you,
And cure your heart of its ache."

The Church's banners are waving,
They are chanting a hymn divine;
'Tis at Cöllen is that procession,
At Cöllen upon the Rhine.

With the throng the mother follows ;
  Her son she leads him ; and now
They both of them sing in the chorus,
  " Ever honoured, O Mary, be thou ! "

II.

The Mother of God at Kevlaar
  Is drest in her richest array ;
She has many a cure on hand there,
  Many sick folk come to her to-day.

And her, for their votive offerings,
  The suffering sick folk greet
With limbs that in wax are moulded,
  Many waxen hands and feet.

And whoso a wax hand offers,
  His hand is healed of its sore ;
And whoso a wax foot offers,
  His foot it will pain him no more.

To Kevlaar went many on crutches
  Who now on the tight-rope bound,
And many play now on the fiddle
  Had there not one finger sound.

The mother she took a wax taper,
   And of it a heart she makes :
" Give that to the Mother of Jesus,
   She will cure thee of all thy aches."

With a sigh her son took the wax heart,
   He went to the shrine with a sigh ;
His words from his heart trickle sadly,
   As trickle the tears from his eye.

" Thou blest above all that are blessed,
   Thou virgin unspotted, divine,
Thou Queen of the Heavens, before thee
   I lay all my anguish and pine.

" I lived with my mother at Cöllen,
   At Cöllen in the town that is there,
The town that has hundreds many
   Of chapels and churches fair.

" And Gretchen she lived there near us,
   But now she is dead, well-a-day !
O Mary ! a wax-heart I bring thee,
   Heal thou my heart's wound, I pray !

" Heal thou my heart of its anguish,
  And early and late, I vow,
With its whole strength to pray and to sing, too,
  'Ever honour'd, O Mary, be thou!'"

III.

The suffering son and his mother
  In their little bed-chamber slept;
Then the Mother of God came softly,
  And close to the sleepers crept.

She bent down over the sick one,
  And softly her hand did lay
On his heart, with a smile so tender,
  And presently vanish'd away.

The mother sees all in her dreaming,
  And other things too she mark'd;
Then up from her slumber she waken'd,
  So loudly the town dogs bark'd.

There lay her son, to his full length
  Stretch'd out, and he was dead;
And the light on his pale cheek flitted
  Of the morning's dawning red.

She folded her hands together,
   She felt as she knew not how,
And softly she sang and devoutly,
   "Ever honour'd, O Mary, be thou!"

FROM THE TOUR IN THE HARZ

1824

PROLOGUE.

COAL-BLACK dress-coats, silken stockings,
  Courtly ruffles, snowy-fair,
Oily speeches, smiles, embracings—
  Ah, if only hearts were there!

Hearts within the breasts, and hot love
  Coursing hotly through the veins ;—
Oh, it kills me, all their whining
  O'er fictitious lovers' pains!

To the mountains I will clamber,
  Where the huts of good men be,
Where the soul expands in freedom,
  Where the winds are blowing free.

To the mountains I will clamber,
  Where the dark pines cleave the sky,
Where brooks brawl, and birds are singing
  And the clouds sweep proudly by.

Fare-ye-well, ye polished *salons*,
  Polished dames and lords, awhile ;
To the mountains I will clamber,
  Thence look down on you and smile !

ON THE HARDENBERG.

BURST, O heart, thy stony cerements!
Dreams of long ago arise!
Songs of rapture, tears of anguish
Gush forth, gush in wondrous wise.

I will ramble through the pinewood,
Where the living brooklet springs,
Where the forest monarch wanders,
Where the winsome throstle sings.

Up the mountain I will clamber,
To the rifted crags away,
Where the morning's flush is kindling
Round the castle's ruins grey.

There I'll sit me down and ponder
On the days of old,—on all
The lordly knights and lovely ladies,
Vanished long from bower and hall.

Grass has overgrown the tilt-yard,
  Where the castle's haughty lord
Kept the lists against all comers,—
  Won the victor's proud award.

Ivy coils about the window,
  Where the Queen of Beauty stood,
Who the imperious all-subduer
  With her lovely eyes subdued.

Ah! the hand of Death has conquered
  Conquering dame and conquering knight;
Low in dust that grizzly mower
  Lays us all, howe'er we fight.

MOUNTAIN IDYL.

I.

ON the mountain stands the cottage
 Of the good old mountaineer,
Where the green pine sighs and rustles,
 And the golden moon shines clear

In the cottage stands an arm-chair,
 Carved with cunning, quaint and high;
Happy is the man that fills it,
 And that happy man am I!

On the stool a girl is seated,
 On my knee her arms repose;
Eyes like twin blue stars, a dainty
 Mouth like any crimson rose.

And those sweet blue stars, as large as
 Heaven itself, upon me gaze;
And her lily finger archly
 On that crimson rose she lays.

No !—the mother does not see us,
   For she's spinning might and main ;
And the father to his zither
   Stoutly sings an old-world strain ;

And the little maiden whispers
   Soft, with 'bated breath, and low ;—
Many a secret she already
   Has to me confided so :

" Since my auntie died, we cannot
   Fare, as once we used to fare,
To the Wappenschaw at Goslar ;—
   Oh, it's quite too lovely there !

" But, ah me ! it is so lonely
   On these high bleak hills, you know ;
And in winter time we're buried—
   Yes, we are—among the snow ;

" And I'm but a timid maiden,
   Frightened like a very child
At the wicked mountain spirits,
   Who at night go ranging wild !"

Then, as though her own words scared her,
  Suddenly she stops, the dear;
And upon her eyes she presses
  Both her tiny hands in fear.

Outside louder sighs the pine-tree,
  And the wheel goes whirring on;
Twangs the zither, and the father
  Croons his chant of ages gone.

"Evil spirits may not harm you;
  Fear not, sweet, what they can do!
Day and night, dear child, the angels
  Watch are keeping over you!"

II.

Taps with fingers green the pine-tree
  At the casement small and mean,
And the moon, the silent warder,
  Through it flings her golden sheen.

In the next room, father, mother,
  Both a-bed, are fast asleep;
But we two with blissful prattle
  Wide awake each other keep.

" Ah, you scarcely will persuade me,
　You too often say your pray'rs !—
Never on your lips from praying
　Came that ugly twitch of theirs !

" Oh, that twitch !—so cold, so wicked !
　Every time, it makes me start,
Till your eyes, so clear, so kindly,
　Take the load from off my heart !

" That you have belief, or any
　Worth the name, I doubt almost !
Have you faith in God the Father,
　In the Son, and Holy Ghost ?"

" Ah, my child, while yet a stripling
　By my mother's knee I stood,
I believed in God the Father,
　Throned on high, the Great and Good !—

" Who created this fair earth, and
　Men, that fair and glorious are—
Who their destined course appointed
　To each sun, and moon, and star !

" As I grew, child, and my reason
　　Ever wider limits won,
Deeper thinking, feeling, taught me
　　To believe, too, in the Son—

" That dear Son, who, in the fulness
　　Of His love, showed love to us,
And, for thanks, was by the people
　　Crucified—'tis always thus !

" Now to manhood grown, read deeply,
　　Travelled wide from pole to pole,
Meekly in the Holy Spirit
　　I believe with all my soul !

" It has wrought the mightiest marvels ;
　　Mightier still is working now ;
It has stormed the tyrants' strongholds,
　　Burst the bondman's yoke, I trow ;

" Healed all wounds, however deadly ;
　　The primeval law renewed,
That all men by birth are equal—
　　Scions of a noble brood.

" It dispels the mists malignant,
  And the phantoms dark that blight
All our loves, and all our pleasures,
  Mock and flout us day and night!

" Countless knights the Holy Spirit
  To fulfil its high behests
Forth hath sent equipped for battle,
  And with daring fired their breasts !

" Lightning flashes from their falchions,
  Their good banners fan the breeze—
Ah, my child, you fain would look on
  Knights of mettle such as these !

" Well, then, look on me, my darling;
  Kiss me, eye me without fear;
For even such a knight, believe me,
  Of the Holy Ghost is here !"

III.

Silently the moon is setting
  There behind the pine without,
And the lamp burns low beside us,
  Scattering feeblest rays about.

But my twin blue stars burn brightly,
  Flashing forth in fuller blaze,
And the rosebud's crimson kindles,
  And the girl, sweet darling, says :

" Mannikins, wee tiny creatures,
  Steal our bread and bacon.   Yes !
Though it's full at night, by morning
  Not a scrap is in the press.

" From our milk these weeny creatures
  Sip the cream, and, for our pains,
Leave the covers off the dishes,
  So the cat laps what remains.

" And the cat's a witch ; at midnight,
  When the storm is up, she'll creep
To the Witches' Mountain yonder,
  To the great old ruined keep !

" There once stood a mighty castle,
  Full of mirth and trumpets' blare ;
Glittering knights and squires and ladies
  Trod their stately measures there.

" Then a mighty sorceress cursed them—
  Castle, inmates—yes, indeed !
So 'tis nothing now but ruins,
  Where the owlets build and breed.

" Yet, if one can speak the proper
  Word—so poor dear auntie thought—
At the proper hour of darkness,
  Up there, on the proper spot,—

" Then into a stately castle
  All the ruins turn again,
And again the knights and ladies
  Foot it there with all their train.

" And that word—the man that speaks it
  Lord of keep and all becomes,
And is welcomed to his honours
  With the clash of trumps and drums !"

Thus do fairy pictures blossom
  On those lips of rosy red,
And o'er all those eyes so tender
  Their blue starry lustre shed.

Round my hand the little maiden
  Twines and twines her golden hair,
Gives my fingers pretty names, laughs,
  Kisses them, and pauses there!

All within that quiet chamber
  Such an air familiar wore;
Table, press, methought I'd seen them
  Many and many a time before.

Like a friend the wall-clock prattles,
  And the zither, near by it,
Of itself begins to tinkle,
  And as in a dream I sit.

Now, now is the proper moment,
  And the proper spot is this;
Yes, and now the proper word will
  From my lips escape, I wis.

See, child, how already midnight
  Drawing on begins to quake;
Louder roar the brook and forest,
  The old mountain is awake.

Songs of elves and fairy harping
    From its rifted fissures ring,
And from these a flowery thicket
    Shoots out like a headlong Spring :

Flowers majestic, flowers of marvel,
    Foliage fairy-like and vast,
Flushed and fragrant, all a-shiver
    As though stirred by passion's blast.

Roses wild as ruddy fire-flakes
    From the medley flash on high ;
Lilies fair as crystal pillars
    Shoot aloft into the sky.

And the stars look down with yearning,
    Looming large as suns ; in showers
Streams their diamond radiance downwards
    On the lily's giant flowers.

But far greater transformation
    O'er ourselves has come, my dear :
Silks and gold and flashing torchlight
    Gaily gleam around us here.

14

Thou'rt a princess grown, this cottage
　　Turned into thy castle fair ;
Knights and dames and squires make merry,
　　Tread their stately measures there.

But of thee and all, retainers,
　　Castle, lord have I become,
And I'm welcomed to my honours
　　With the clash of trump and drum!

" König ist der Hirtenknabe."

THE herd-boy is a king, his throne
 Is a breadth of hill and down,
The sun that shines above him
 Is his glorious golden crown.

About his feet the sheep lie,
 Smooth flatterers, cross'd with red ;
The calves are the equerries,
 And strut with haughty tread.

The goats are the court comedians ;
 The birds, and cows at hand,
With their flutings, and their tinklings,
 Are His Majesty's private band.

These sing and ting-ting so sweetly,
 And cadence so sweetly keep
To the waterfall and the pine-trees,
 That they lull the king to sleep.

And while he sleeps, yon sheep-dog,
　　As First Minister, plays the king,
And he makes his growls and barkings
　　All round and round him ring.

The young king moans, half dreaming:
　　"To rule is so hard!　Oh me,
I wish, that at home with only
　　My own queen I might be!

"Upon her bosom pillowed
　　My head so softly lies,
And I find a realm unbounded
　　In her bewitching eyes!"

[Heine introduces this poem in his "Harz Reise"
thus: "It was mid-day when I came upon one of
the herds of cattle which are found among these hills;
and the herd-boy, a good-natured, fair young fellow,
told me that the great mountain, at whose base I was
standing, was the old world-renowned Brocken.　There
is not a house for miles round, and I was glad enough
to be invited by the young man to share his meal.
Down we sat to a *déjeûner-dinatoire*, consisting of
cheese and bread; the lambkins nibbled the crumbs,
the dear stupid calves frisked round about us, and

tinkled roguishly with their little bells, and laughed at us with their great contented eyes. We fared right royally; above all, mine host appeared to me to be a real king; and as he is the only king who up to this time has given me bread, I have a mind to sing of him also in royal wise."]

ON THE BROCKEN.

SEE, where now the east is kindling,
  By the coming sunbeams kissed!
Far and wide the mountain summits
  Float upon the sea of mist.

If the seven-league boots were mine now,
  Swifter than the wind I'd fleet
Over yonder mountain summits
  To the home that holds my sweet.

Softly would I draw the curtains,
  Where she lies in sleep's eclipse,
Kiss her softly on the forehead,
  Softly kiss her ruby lips ;

And still softlier would I whisper
  In her little lily ear,
" Dream, dream on, that we are lovers,
  And have ne'er been parted, dear."

THE PRINCESS ILSE.

[This poem should be read after the passage of prose
poetry by which it is preceded in the "Harz Reise."
"It is impossible to describe with what sprightliness,
naïveté, and grace the Ilse dashes over the confusedly-
tumbled rocks which she encounters in her course—the
water in one place hissing up wildly or breaking into
foam, in another gushing in perfect curves out of all sorts
of fissures in the stones, as out of so many brimming
flagons—and then again tripping down below over the
pebble-stones like a frolicsome girl. Yes, the Saga is
true, that the Ilse is a princess, who runs down the
mountain laughing and in the full bloom of beauty!
How her white robe of foam gleams in the sunlight!
How the silvery ribbons of her bodice flutter in the
wind! How her diamonds blaze and sparkle! The
lofty beeches stand along her path, like grave fathers,
that contemplate with suppressed smiles the wayward-
ness of their darling child; the white birches wave
with an aunt-like complacency, and yet not unmingled

with concern, at her venturesome leaps; the haughty
oak looks like a morose uncle, who has to pay the piper
for these vagaries; the little birds in the air carol their
admiration; the flowers along the banks whisper softly,
'Oh take us with you, take us with you, sister dear!' But
on bounds the merry maiden without stopping, and all
at once she is caught by the dreaming poet, and down
upon me streams a flowery rain of musical radiance
and of radiant music; I am lost in a transport of pure
delight, and I still hear only the voice of flute-like
sweetness, which says:—]

I AM the Princess Ilse,
   And I dwell at the Ilsenstein;
Come with me to my castle,
   And bliss shall be thine and mine.

With the cool of my glass-clear waters
   Thy brow and thy locks I'll lave;
And thou'lt think of thy sorrows no longer,
   For all that thou look'st so grave.

With my white arms twined around thee,
   And lapped on my breast so white,
Thou shalt lie, and dream of elf-land—
   Its loves and its wild delight.

I will kiss thee, love, and caress thee,
   As once I kissed and caressed
That dear old Kaiser Heinrich,
   Who's dead now, and gone to rest.

The dead keep dead, and the living,
   They live and only they;
And I am bonnie and blooming,
   My heart leaps and laughs alway.

Come down with me to my castle,
   To my halls of the crystal sheen ;
There ladies and knights are dancing,
   And the squires make merry between.

There is rustling of silken raiment,
   And clinking of spurs of steel ;
With horn, drum, trump, and fiddle,
   The dwarfs make the dancers wheel.

But my arms in their clasp shall fold thee,
   As they did Kaiser Heinrich too ;
I stopped up his ears with caresses,
   Whenever the trumpet blew."

MISCELLANEOUS

LOVE'S BURIAL.

THOU hast passed from life, and thou knowest it
 not;
The light is quenched in thine eyes, I wot;
Thy rose-red mouth, it is wan and sere,
And thou art dead, my poor dead dear!

One summer night, myself I saw
Thee laid in earth with a shuddering awe;
The nightingales fluted low dirge-like lays,
And the stars came out on thy bier to gaze.

As the mourning train through the wood defiles
Their litany peals up the branching aisles;
The pine-trees, in funeral mantles dressed,
Moan prayers for the soul that is gone to rest.

And as by the mountain tarn we wound,
The elves were dancing a fairy round;
They stopped, and they seemed, though startled thus,
With looks of pity to gaze at us.

And when we came to thy lone earth-bed,
The moon came down from the heaven o'erhead.
She spoke of the lost one. A sob, a stound!
And the bells in the far-away distance sound.

A FIRESIDE PIECE.

OUTSIDE the blast is making riot,
  And through the darkness the snowflakes fall;
Here in my little room all is quiet,
  Warm and dry, and so snug withal.

Musing I sit on my cushioned settle,
  Facing the firelight's fitful shine;
Sings on the hob the simmering kettle,
  Songs that seem echoes of "auld lang syne."

And close beside me the cat sits purring,
  Warming her paws at the cheery gleam;
The flames keep flitting, and flicking, and whirring,—
  My mind is lapped in a realm of dream.

Many long, long forgotten summers
  Rise up, wraith-like, before my view,
Some in the brightness of masking mummers,
  Some with their splendours bedimmed in hue.

Lovely, serene-faced women sweetly
  Meanings divine in a glance convey;
Revellers, mingling among them fleetly,
  Caper and laugh, and are madly gay.

Marble gods in the distance tower;
  Near them, dream-like in beauty rare,
Is a fairy grove that has burst in flower,
  And sheds perfume on the moonlit air.

Castles full many of wizard story
  Totter along with their crests awry;
Knights behind them, in full-plumed glory,
  With troops of their squires come riding by.

'Tis gone!   The beautiful dream is over!
  Away like a phantom the pageant draws!
Oh dear!   The kettle is boiling over,
  And pussy is yelling with scalded paws.

" Der Schmetterling ist in die Rose verliebt."

THE butterfly is with the rose in love,
　Flits round her all the day;
But round himself with a fondling smile
　The passion-stricken sunbeams play.

With whom the while is the rose in love?
　Who knows what her secrets are?
Is it the full-throated nightingale?
　Is it the silent evening star?

I know not with whom the rose is in love,
　But I love you all *sans* fail,
Rose, and sunbeams, and butterfly,
　Evening star, and nightingale.

" Die blaue Frühling's Augen."

THE azure eyes of spring-time
    Look up from the grass; and they
Are the violets sweet I have chosen
    As a posie for my dear May.

I gather them, thinking, thinking,
    And all the thoughts that crowd
On my heart, and set it sighing,
    The nightingale sings aloud.

Yes, all I think she sings out
    In loud and piercing tone;
So is my tender secret
    To all the woodland known.

" Wenn du vorüberwandelst."

IF thou dost but pass before me,
  And I feel but the touch of thy dress,
My heart shouts, and follows in rapture
  The track of thy loveliness.

Then thou turnest about, and bendest
  Those great eyes of thine on me,
And my heart is so stricken with panic,
  It scarcely can follow thee.

" Dass du mich liebst, das wusst' ich."

OH yes! I knew you loved me,
   Long since I divined it well;
But when to myself you owned it,
   Great fear upon me fell.

Away I rushed to the mountains,
   I shouted and sang for glee;
I went to the beach and wept there,
   Till the sun went down in the sea.

My heart, it is, even as the sun is,
   All flame to the gazer's sight;
And it sets in a sea of love, too,
   Majestical and bright.

" Schattenküsse, Schattenliebe."

STRANGE, you say, that life, love, kisses
    Are but shadows!   Ah! do you
Think, you little goose, all bliss is
    Changeless and for ever true?

Things that to the soul seem nearest
    Leave us, looming less and less;
Hearts forget, and eyes the dearest
    Drowse in loveless listlessness.

" Mit Schwarzen Segeln segelt mein Schiff."

WITH inky sails my pinnace drives
    Across the stormy sea;
You know how wretched I am, and yet
  So cruelly torture me.

Your heart is faithless as the wind,
  As fickle as heart may be;
With inky sails my pinnace drives
  Across the stormy sea.

" Es ragt tüs Meer der Runenstein."

I SIT on the Runenstein and dream,
　With the sea-waves round me plashing;
The wind it whistles, the sea-mews scream,
　The billows are foaming and dashing.

Fair girls a many loved have I,
　And many good worthy fellows;
Where are they now?—The wind whistles high,
　And on sweep the foaming billows.

" Das Meer erstrahlt im Sonnenschein."

THE sea is shining in the sun,
    As though of gold it were ;
When I am dead, dear comrades,
    Take me and sink me there.

The sea was ever so dear to me,
    Its waters softly fell
Like balm on my heart so often ;
    We loved each other well.

THE NETHER WORLD.

I.

" MY bachelor days that I might recall!"
    Says Pluto oft with a deep-drawn sigh.
" In this plaguy state of wedlock I
Find that of yore, when I had no wife,
Hell was truly no hell at all.

"Oh, my bachelor days that I might recall!
Ever since Proserpine shared my bed,
No day but I've wish'd that I were dead;
I can't hear my Cerberus bark, when she
Takes in her head to squabble and squall.

" In vain I struggle my whole life through
For quiet.   Here in this realm of gloom
No damnèd sprite has so hard a doom;
I envy Sisyphus' self, and those
Plucky Danaus girls, I do!"

II.

In the realm of shades, on a throne of gold,
Beside her royal lord, behold
    Fair Proserpine ! Dark
    Is her brow, and, mark !
Sadly thus to herself she sighs :

" I pant for roses, I pant for the gush
Of wood-birds' songs, for the sun's warm flush ;
    And here 'mid hosts
    Of Lemurs and ghosts
My young life withers and wastes and dies.

"To the yoke of wedlock I'm chain'd and bound
In this hideous rat*hole underground,
    Where spectres thin
    After dark look in
At my window, and Styx make ceaseless moan.

" I've ask'd old Charon to dine to-night ;
But he's bald, and his legs have no calves, the fright !
    The judges too come,
    Long-visaged and glum ;
Amid such a set I must turn to stone ! "

III.

While such grievances are piling
   Up within the world below,
Ceres on the earth the while in
   Frantic grief runs to and fro;
Trapesing without cap or collar
   Up and down the country through,
Moaning out those words of dolour,
   So well known[1] to all of you:

"Is this sweet Spring reappearing?
   Is this earth grown young once more?
Green the hills are, sunlit, cheering,
   Winter's icy reign is o'er.
Streamlets blue, that glide unruffled,
   Mirror back unclouded skies;
Soft the breezes blow, and muffled,
   Buds begin to ope their eyes;
Songs in every grove awaken,
   And the Oread whispers—See,
Back are come the flowers,—forsaken
   Has thy daughter them and thee!

---

[1] Well known indeed; for the next three stanzas are taken bodily from Schiller's famous "Lament of Ceres."

"Oh the weary hours I've wander'd
  O'er the earth from place to place !
Titan, all thy rays I've squander'd,
  Seeking my beloved to trace.
Tidings of my darling daughter
  No one yet to me has brought ;
Day, that finds out all, has sought her,
  My lost dear, but found her not.
Say, from me, Zeus, hast thou torn her?
  Madden'd by her charms supreme,
Can the lord of hell have borne her
  Down to Orcus' rueful stream ?

"Who will carry my bewailing
  Hence to yonder gloomy strand ?
Ever is the grim bark sailing,
  But with shadows only mann'd.
Living eye has brooded never
  Those night-mantled meadows o'er,
And since Styx has been a river,
  Living freight it never bore.
Countless steps lead down, I ween, there,
  But not one leads back to day ;
No one, who her tears has seen there,
  Can the woful tale convey."

IV.

" Dear dame Ceres, don't distress ye,
    Drop your moaning, drop your prayer !
Your heart's wish I'll grant, and, bless ye !
    I too have had much to bear.

" Be consoled ! We'll part her fairly,
    Your dear girl, between us twain ;
And for six months she shall yearly
    In the upper world remain.

" Aid thee there in summer hours
    In your tasks of field and farm ;
Wear a hat of straw, with flowers
    Stuck all round it for a charm.

" Grow ecstatic, when eve flushes
    All the sky with ruddy rose,
And his pipe beside the rushes
    Some chaw-bacon sweetly blows.

" At the harvest-home her glee will
    Vie with that of Joe and Jess ;
'Mongst the sheep and goslings she will
    Prove herself a lioness.

"Oh the peace beyond describing!
  I the while can live my life,
Punch with Lethe mix'd imbibing,
  All oblivious of my wife !"

THE SLAVE SHIP.

I.

THE supercargo, Mynheer van Koek,
  In his cabin sits, and counts up
His profits to come, and he smiles to see
  How the tot of the ship's load mounts up.

" The spices are good, and the pepper is good,
  Sacks, barrels three hundred of crack stuff;
Then there are the gold and the ivory;—
  But better than all is the black stuff.

" Six hundred niggers in barter I took,
  Dog-cheap on the Senegal river;
Their flesh is firm, their sinews like steel,
  Of the best brand our makers deliver.

" Brandy I gave in exchange for them,
  Glass beads, and cutlers' gear, too;
If only one half of them live, I gain
  One hundred per cent—all clear, too.

" Even say, three hundred negroes are all
  We've left us at Rio Janeiro,
They'll fetch me a hundred ducats per head
  From the house of Gonzalez Pereiro."

He had got so far, when Mynheer van Koek
  Had his cheery dream broken in on
By the cutter's surgeon walking in,
  Doctor Avish M'Tavish M'Kinnon.

A stick of a man, on whose blazing nose
  Full many a red wart figures;—
" Now, my surgeon-in-chief," exclaims Van Koek,
  " How get on my darling niggers?"

" Thanks, thanks for inquiries," the doctor says;
  " I came to say, overnight, sir,
The mortality 'mongst them has mounted up
  In a way that's exceptional quite, sir.

" Amidships they always died two a-day,
  But last night seven of them hooked it,—
Four men, three women—that's the loss,
  I've been to the day-book, and booked it.

" Their bodies, I tested and tried them well;
   For these rascals—don't I know them?—
Often sham to be dead, on the simple chance
   That into the sea we throw them.

" I took the irons off their limbs,
   And, as I commonly do, sir,
Their bodies, as soon as the sun was up,
   Clean overboard I threw, sir.

" In an instant up shot a swarm of sharks
   From below to overhaul them :
They are so fond of the negro beef;
   My pensioners I call them !

" They have followed the ship's wake ever since
   We left the coasting station ;
The creatures sniff up the carcass smell
   With epicure exultation.

" To see them snap at the dead men is
   As pretty a sight as one knows of !
One seizes a head, another a leg,
   What is left the others dispose of !

" When they've cleared off all, they go tumbling round
    The ship, quite contented and happy,
And they leer at me, with a look that says,
    ' A capital breakfast, old chap, eh ! ' "

But here, with a sigh, Van Koek breaks in ;
    " How to get this mischief under?
This dreadful mortality, how am I
    To arrest its growth, I wonder?"

The doctor answers : " The fault's their own,
    These niggers drop off so quickly ;
Their own bad breath has made the air
    Between decks horribly sickly.

" Many have died, too, of doleful dumps,
    Too deadly dull to endure them :
By a trifle of music and dancing and air
    Let us of their megrims cure them."

Then cries Van Koek, " Good sound advice !
    My medical staff commander
Is sage as Aristotle himself,
    The tutor of Alexander.

"The President of the Society
    For tulip-culture in Delft, sir,
Is clever—very—but not by half
    So clever as yourself, sir.

"Ho! music! music!   These black knaves
    Shall here on the deck cut capers;
And those who decline, the cat-o'-nine
    Shall quickly cure of the vapours."

II.

High in the great blue vault of heaven
    Many thousand stars were gleaming,
So wistful-sad, so large and calm,
    Like the eyes of beautiful women.

They are looking down upon the sea,
    That is veiled in a phosphorescent
Vapour for miles of a purple tinge;
    The waves make a murmur pleasant.

No sail flaps on the slaver's ship,
    As 'twere dismantled it lies there;
But lanterns shine on the quarter-deck,
    And the sounds of music rise there.

The pilot has taken the fiddle in hand,
 The cook on the flute is playing,
A smart young cabin-boy beats the drum,
 On the horn is the doctor braying.

Some hundred negroes, women and men,
 Halloo, and caper, and wheel round,
As though they were mad ; and their iron gyves
 Beat steady time as they reel round.

They stamp the deck with insane delight ;
 And many a swarthy fair, too,
In transport her naked partner clasps,—
 And oh, the groans that are there too !

The mate is *mâitre des plaisirs*,
 And the laggard dancers he has
Quickened with strokes of his cat-o'-nine
 To friskier ideas.

And Diddle-dum-dey and Tootle-te-too ;
 The din lures up from the deep there
The monsters of the watery world,
 That drowse in a fatuous sleep there.

16

Hundreds and hundreds of sharks swim by,
　　Possessed by a dreamy distraction,
And up at the ship they glower and blink
　　In a maze of stupefaction.

They're quite aware that the breakfast-hour
　　Has not arrived, and their jaws are
With yawning agape, one can see them set
　　With teeth as thickly as saws are.

And Diddle-dum-dey and Tootle-te-too—
　　Such endless dancing and setting,
The sharks in sheer impatience the while
　　Their teeth on their own tails whetting.

I trow they love not music, they,
　　And, like most of their kidney, show it;
"Trust no one that does not music love !"
　　Said Albion's greatest poet.

And Tootle-te-too and Diddle-dum-dey,
　　The dancing it goes on stoutly;
By the fore-mast stands Mynheer van Koek,
　　And he folds his hands devoutly.

"For Jesu's sake, spare, Lord, the lives
  Of these black sinners, spare them !
If they've angered Thee, ah, well Thou know'st,
  To swine we may compare them.

"Oh, spare their lives, for Jesu's sake,
  That all us mortals died for ;
For unless three hundred head survive
  I lose every stiver I tried for!"

A MEETING.

ALL under the lime-trees the music sounds,
  And lads and lasses dance there, too;
A couple are dancing whom no one knows,
  They are tall, and of noble air, too.

To and fro, in a weird-like way,
  They glide and meander slowly;
They smile to each other, they wave their heads,
  The lady whispers lowly:

" My fine young fellow, in your cap
  A water-pink is twined, sir;
It only grows at the roots of the sea,—
  You come not of Adam's kind, sir.

" You are a Merman; to beguile
  These village beauties you wish, eh ?
I knew you at the very first glance
  By your teeth so sharp and fishy."

To and fro, in a weird-like way,
    They glide and meander slowly;
They smile to each other, they wave their heads,
    The young man whispers lowly :

" My pretty maiden, tell me why
    As cold as ice your hand is?
Ay, tell me why your white robe's hem
    As moist as the wet sea sand is?

" I knew you at the very first
    By your curtsey all so tricksy;—
No mortal child of earth are you,
    You are my cousin, the Nixie."

The fiddles are silent, the dance is done,
    They part with a courtly greeting ;
They know each other, alas! too well,
    So shun any future meeting.

THE EXORCISM.

THE young Franciscan sits alone
   Within his cloister-cell,
He reads an old magician's book,
  'Tis call'd " The Stress of Hell."

And when the hour of midnight strikes,
  He can curb himself no mo';
With pale, pale lips he calls upon
  The powers of the world below:

" Ye spirits ! fetch me from the grave
  The fairest of womankind;
Give her life for me just this one night,
  'Twill edify my mind."

He speaks the exorcism dread,
  Straightway is his wish complete;
The poor long-buried beauty comes,
  Swathed up in her winding-sheet.

Her look is woe-worn ; from her breast
  Sighs sad with anguish rise ;
She sits down by him, they speak no word,
  And gaze in each other's eyes.

THE VALE OF TEARS.

THE night-wind through the dormers howls,
  And two poor creatures lay
In a garret upon a truckle-bed,
  And wasted and wan were they.

And one unto the other says:
  "Oh, gather me into your arm,
And press your lips, dear, close to mine,
  I want you to make me warm."

And this is what the other says:
  "When I look into your eyes,
Hunger and cold and want are forgot,
  All my earthly trouble flies."

Much did they kiss, they wept still more,
  Clasp'd hand to hand, and sigh'd,
They laugh'd very often, and even sang,
  Then their talk into silence died.

Next morning the police inspector came,
  And there by that woful bed
He with the parish doctor stood,
  Who certified both were dead.

"The cruel weather," said his report,
  "Combined with inanition,
Has caused the collapse of both,—at least,
  Has hastened that condition."

When frosts set in, he went on to say,
  'Tis vital the body should
Be protected by woollen blankets—likewise
  Be nourished by wholesome food.

www.ingramcontent.com/pod-product-compliance
Lightning Source LLC
Chambersburg PA
CBHW020343030726
47496CB00007B/1981